The BERLIN AFFAIR

Stephanie Smith

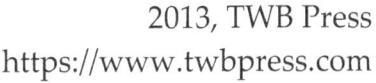

2013, TWB Press
https://www.twbpress.com

The Berlin Affair
Copyright © 2013 by Stephanie Smith

Edited by Terry Wright

Cover Art by Terry Wright

Published by Amore Moon Publishing, an imprint of TWB Press. www.twbpress.com

ISBN 978-1-936991-60-0

Chapter ONE

My darling Marianne,
You are my light, my breath, my very soul.
To hold you in my arms is my only comfort. My only desire.
With you at my side we can conquer any challenge that befalls us.
I love you. I will love you forever.

MARIANNE TUCKER CRUMPLED up the old love letter and tossed it over her shoulder. "Blech. Enough of that."

The wad landed behind her, near the growing heap of letters on the floor. She couldn't seem to concentrate on anything lately. And now this recent discovery of a set of old love letters became a painful reminder of Jake, which only added misery to her memories of him, what he'd done to her, and the painful scar he'd left on her heart. Maybe this upcoming change of scene would be just what she needed.

Morning sunrays pouring through the window made her feel like a cat in need of a good stretch. She arched her back and stretched her arms toward the ceiling. "I'm so done with you, Jake." Lowering her arms, she stood, grabbed her last packed bag, and dragged it to the front door then strolled into her well-organized kitchen.

Glancing around, she prided herself in keeping everything perfectly in place. Gleaming copper pots and pans hung on the wall from the smallest saucepan to the largest skillet. Her whole life was like this kitchen, completely organized and well-managed. Well, except her love life. That was a disaster.

She poured water into the top of the coffee-maker and watched the brewing coffee drip into the pot and fog up the glass.

A flash of light flickered on the wall. Turning around, she discovered the source of the light, a crystal ornament dangling by a thread in the window. She remembered the day she received the gift from her cousin, Sharon. They had aged ten years since then.

Curious about what all that time had done to her, she moved to the hallway mirror and inspected her reflection for any telltale wrinkles. At twenty-eight, her 5'8" figure still looked trim in spite of having gained a few pounds. Her blue sundress accented her long golden hair, which fluttered easily from her shoulders to her waist. She smiled at her reflection—

A loud clatter spun her around just in time to find Sharon dumping a heavy load of groceries on the kitchen counter. "Sorry. I didn't mean to startle you." She picked up a can that had spilled out of a bag. The way her face was crinkled, she looked worried that Marianne would be upset over this less-than-quiet arrival. She'd been a little moody these days. "Guess you didn't hear me come in."

Marianne returned to the kitchen. "I was just thinking about how old I'm getting."

"You're still gorgeous. Don't worry about it."

"I could have been married by now. Had a couple kids..."

Sharon put the can in a cupboard. "It's Jake's loss." She wrapped her slender arms around Marianne's shoulders. "You sure you still want to go through with this move to Berlin?" Her voice was filled with concern. "There's still time to change your mind. I'm sure your boss would take you back in a second."

"I'm going." Marianne's answer sounded full of determination. "Like the song says, my bags are packed and I'm ready to go."

"Yeah, you've been keeping to yourself for too long anyway."

Marianne watched the light dance off the dangling crystal in the window. She liked the job she just quit. Her boss had always admired her work, and he had rewarded her with a promotion and a generous raise. She felt proud of the way she had worked up through the company's ranks, first being a data entry clerk, then moving up the tech ladder to become a computer programmer and comptroller. It was hard to walk away from that accomplishment, but her memories of the life she'd lived in San Diego, the love she'd lost, had to be left behind somehow. Her eyes misted.

"Hey, hello in there. Anybody home?" Sharon's

excited chatter broke into Marianne's thoughts. "Are you sure I can't come with you? I could be your assistant." Sharon's eyes glimmered with envy.

Marianne knew the two of them could have so much fun together, but: "I've got to do this alone." She pointed to the groceries on the counter. "While you put those away, I'll pour us some coffee."

"I'll have mine black."

While Marianne lined up two coffee cups, Sharon focused on her task, stocking the cabinets. Her green eyes glowed with excitement. "Wow. A Foreign Service Officer. Your new job sounds so mysterious and romantic." Lowering her voice and looking from left to right, and then focusing her gaze on Marianne, she whispered, "Are you going to be a spy or something?"

A giggle burbled from Marianne's lips. "No, Silly." She picked up the coffee pot. "I'm not going to be a spy. I'm going to work at the American Consulate. It's a boring desk job in the passport office."

A few months back, Marianne had decided a change in career and locale would be good for her, and on a friend's advice, she took the Foreign Service Exam. Much to her delight, her high scores had her rushing to Washington, DC, where a hundred other qualified applicants competed for a few positions. For several days, she was tested and questioned and investigated, and before she knew it, she was offered a job in Berlin. Holy cow, of all places: Berlin...the capital of Germany, smack dab behind the Iron

Curtain. What better place on earth could there have been for her to forget Jake and mend her broken heart? She remembered grinning as she signed the final acceptance paperwork for the job. This would be a good change of pace for her. An adventure to be certain, and in the end, maybe even a new love.

She poured two steaming cups and passed one to Sharon.

Sharon placed it on the table in front of her. "I'll wait for it to cool down a bit."

Marianne reached into the cupboard and grabbed a box of Girl Scout cookies. She bit into one then sipped hot coffee. Her thoughts began to wander. Although she felt sad to leave her friends and family, she eagerly looked forward to her new life. After all, she was pushing thirty, and she wanted to experience a bit more...no, a *lot more* of life. Jake had nearly knocked the will to live out of her.

"Did you read the news today?" Sharon held up the newspaper. Her eyes filled with concern as she briefly scanned an article. "Somebody got shot while trying to go over the Berlin Wall."

Marianne squinted. "Let me see."

"Page 2A." Sharon handed over the newspaper.

Marianne set down her cup and examined the paper's date: February 7, 1989. Her eyes quickly scanned the short but disturbing article about a young man who was shot to death by four East German guards while trying to escape East Berlin. A shiver of dread pulsed through her skin, raising goose bumps. "Pretty scary stuff." She hoped she would never witness the violence there.

Worrisome voices crept into her thoughts. *Are you sure you are doing the right thing? Berlin sounds dangerous.* Here in sunny San Diego, she was safe. She had a secure job with an international computer firm, and she could have easily moved into upper management if she had desired. But San Diego wasn't Berlin. And Berlin was far enough away to forget San Diego and what happened here, she hoped.

She furrowed her eyebrows and set the paper on the table. "Please don't worry about me, Sharon, I'll be fine." She sipped her coffee, content about her decision in spite of the violence. Besides, she wasn't going anywhere near that wall.

Sharon blew the steam from her coffee. "What if Jake shows up here looking for you?"

Marianne's hand trembled. She tightened her grip on the cup handle. Troubled memories bubbled up and darkened her mood. Her eyes sought out the rhinestone-framed picture in the hallway of a happy couple in love. She and Jake were snuggled into each other against the backdrop of a sandy beach along a stretch of blue Pacific Ocean. She wondered why she had kept it so long. She should have thrown it out months ago.

"You still love him, don't you," Sharon said.

"Of c-course not." Marianne's voice caught as she fought to keep her tears in check. She didn't like lying to her cousin, but it was better than admitting to the obvious.

But why do I still miss him?

The Berlin Affair

She got up from the table, strolled to the hallway, and gazed at the handsome bronzed man smiling back at her. It was a warm sunny day when they'd posed for that picture. A cool sea breeze had tousled Jake's brown hair, which grew over his ears. How she longed to kiss him once more.

She took the picture off the wall and held it to her heart.

At times, she couldn't sleep, reliving over and over again blissful moments she and Jake had spent together cuddled in each other's arms. How his musical laughter and dancing eyes touched her heart with warmth and love. She longed to be his wife, and was thrilled the moment he had asked her to marry him.

Closing her eyes, she smiled, remembering how warm his hands felt as he lifted her hair and kissed her neck. She loved to feel him so near; the heady mixture of his cologne with his masculine scent always fogged her mind, especially when he breathed in her ear, whispering, "I love you, Marianne."

He had lied. Tunnel vision darkened her view of the man she once loved. He never loved her. He left her. She flung the picture down the hallway; it shattered with a loud crash against the living room wall.

Sharon rushed to her side and embraced her. "Forget about him."

"God knows I've tried." She fought back tears as if they were poison.

"He's not worth all this. You haven't heard a

single word from him since the day before your wedding. Maybe he'll never come back."

"I never want to see him again."

Sharon patted Marianne's back. "You're better off without him."

Frowning, she looked at the mess in the corner. Shards of glass lay everywhere. "I don't think Jake ever really cared about me. What do you think?"

"He left you standing at the altar, the prick. And you never heard from him again. What do you think I think? He only cared about himself."

"I hate him."

Sighing, Sharon helped Marianne back to her chair in the kitchen, scooted over another chair, and began to braid her hair. Marianne enjoyed the attention, even when they were children, braiding each other's hair and talking about boys. Who knew it would ever come to this, talking about men and heartbreak?

Sharon shook her head. "What's done is done. We can't change the past." Then tossing a glance in the direction of the broken glass, she added, "Besides, it's not like you to get this angry."

"You're right." Marianne rubbed her teary eyes.

Sharon finished the braid. "There, feel better now?"

"The truth is, a part of me hates him. Another part loves him. And I still need answers so I can have closure. If I ever see Jake again, he'll have a lot of explaining to do."

"What could he possibly say to justify what he

did to you?"

"I don't know." Marianne looked into Sharon's eyes. "Do you think I'm crazy to want to know why he left me like that?"

"It doesn't matter anymore. The best way to get over him is to date someone new."

"But I don't want to get my heart broken again."

"Love is risky business—"

A horn honked outside.

"That's your cab. It's time you get out of here." Her eyes brimmed with tears. She reached over to hug Marianne and ended up squeezing her tight, which started the sobbing all over again. "I'm going to miss you."

"Me too." Marianne hugged her and again had to fight off her own tears.

Sharon broke the embrace and held her at arm's length. "Ready?"

Marianne nodded. Sharon escorted her to the front door where her luggage sat waiting for the adventure to begin.

An impatient toot of the taxi's horn once more brought Sharon to tears.

Marianne hugged her one last time. "I've got to go." She hoisted her suitcases and dragged her carry-on out the door to the waiting driver.

"If you need anything, just write," Sharon called out from the doorway.

"Don't worry. I'm going to have a blast." Marianne got in the back seat, strapped herself in, and looked out the open window as the taxi driver shoved the last piece of luggage into the trunk. Sharon was waving goodbye and crying.

As the taxi pulled away from the curb, Marianne leaned out the window and shouted back at her, "If you hear from Jake, tell him to go to hell for me."

Chapter TWO

HAVING SETTLED IN BERLIN for three weeks, Marianne had stayed busy enough during the workday with her new job to banish Jake from her daily thoughts, but nightly dreams betrayed her true desires:

A gasp froze in Marianne's throat as she saw him kneeling alongside the water's edge. Her heart pounded as her eyes regarded the way his white shorts showed off the tan on his hard-muscled thighs. She wanted to run her fingertips down his muscular back and feel his smooth skin deeply bronzed by endless hours in the sun. The sight of him made her head dizzy with desire.

He remained motionless, gazing across the blue-green bay as if engrossed in far-away thoughts. The sea breeze wisped his brown hair to and fro. She longed to rake her fingers through its thickness.

She approached him cautiously, desperate to appease her curiosity. Was this the man she thought he was? And why did she want him so?

As if he had heard her soft footsteps in the sand behind him, he stood, turned his back to the sparkling water, and gazed at her with longing eyes. It was Jake, all right. A hint of a smile tilted the corners of his mouth. He didn't seem surprised to see her, as if he had been waiting for her all this time.

Her heart started to melt. She swallowed hard. By the way his brown eyes smoldered at the sight of her, she knew her heart was in big trouble.

She spun around and ran away, but his powerful, long strides brought him to her side. His hand caught her arm, stopping her. He placed his palms on her trembling shoulders, held her at arm's length, and forced her to look at him.

Like a small bird, she stood hypnotized in his powerful gaze.

A cry from a seagull overhead broke the spell, allowing her eyes to break contact with his. But his fragrance intoxicated her and sharpened all her senses.

He demanded her complete attention.

She looked up at him. His eyes burned with raw desire and caused her to feel faint and breathless. His muscular chest tapered down to a firm and taut stomach and gave him a powerful sensuality she fought to ignore.

"Jake..." She tried to speak, but in an instant, his strong arms embraced her against his hard chest while his thigh pressed against the sweet spot between her legs, her private place, sending her body temperature aflame.

"My darling," his silky voice breathed in her ear. His lips trailed down across her throat and then moved back up toward her mouth. Her knees buckled as her lips opened to his, and she felt dizzy as his tongue sought hers. She felt as if she was being devoured, and she savored every second of every sensation.

The sea breeze swirling around them became musical. It transported her to a place where there were no worries, no concerns. A wave crashed to shore, sending a carpet of white foam over her toes. The brisk water reminded her to fight for control.

"Jake…please, no." But her body sang a different tune, for long-denied red-hot flames of passion fanned up, threatening to engulf her soul. Once more she fought to resist him, but his insistent kisses and strong embrace had captured her. He was claiming her for his own again. Her resistance slipped away, and her mind grew dim in a fiery pink haze of desire.

As his feverish kisses increased in intensity, Jake's hands slowly moved over her blouse. Her heart raced and her breath became ragged at his touch. And when his fingertips found the rosy tips of her breasts, all common sense came to a screeching halt. Nothing else mattered except her and Jake and this magical moment. But as she breathed the words "I love you" in his ear, he froze, looked at her with a horrified expression, and then suddenly vanished.

Marianne bolted upright in her bed, breathing hard and covered with sweat. Looking quickly about, she breathed a sigh of relief when she recognized the now familiar surroundings of her bedroom. It was just a dream.

But what a dream it was. Oh God...

She placed her hand over her wounded heart and cried out, "Why does he haunt me so?"

Frustration took over. She threw her feather pillow across the room. If only she could get him out of her mind, but not knowing why he'd abandoned her would be the death of her sanity.

Sharon had suggested the best way to get over someone was to date someone new. That was the last thing Marianne wanted right now, another man, a whole new set of problems.

Shopping, yes, that was what she needed.

It was Saturday morning. A trip downtown would put Jake out of her mind.

She tossed off her nightgown and watched it flutter to the floor. Naked like this, she felt a little naughty. Jake was such a fool to leave her. "A hot shower will be nice," she muttered and grabbed a towel on her way to the bathroom.

Her shower controls had hot and cold levers that had to be adjusted to mix the water to the desired temperature. While relaxing under the spray of hot water on her back, the memory of last night's dream bubbled back to the surface. Closing her eyes, she allowed herself to be transported away, and once more, she could smell Jake's sultry scent and feel his body pressed against hers. Sensations pulsed through her belly...and reality struck. Aghast at how her body had reacted, she opened her eyes and reached out to shut off the water. Instead of closing both levers, she accidentally shut off the hot one. The resulting icy shock of cold water racked her body and banished Jake's lust-inducing memory. She shut off the cold water, and shivering, she stepped from the shower stall and wrapped herself in a towel.

"Hmmm…enough of that," she scolded herself, and walked out of the bathroom, thinking about what she would wear for the day.

She padded across the wooden floor, leaving a trail of damp footprints behind, and picked up the feather pillow she had tossed earlier. Hugging it to her towel-wrapped chest, she sat on a padded windowsill seat and peeked outside. The morning sky looked hazy with a promise of an afternoon thundershower. She hadn't gotten accustomed to Berlin's weather yet. One moment it was beautiful and clear, and then before long it was pouring rain. "Well, I'm glad I didn't plan a barbeque today," she muttered.

She picked up a Berlin city map from a nearby end table and flopped on the bed.

Springs groaned.

Lying on her stomach, she unfolded the map and hunted for the downtown area referred to as the Ku'damm, short for Kurfürstendamm. She had read about it in her Berlin welcome packet, which described the area as a favorite place for shopping, sightseeing, and outdoor cafés.

Sounds perfect.

Once she picked out her destination, she noted which subways (known as UBahns) would take her there. With West Berlin surrounded by the Berlin Wall, it would be difficult but not impossible to end up in communist territory by mistake.

Pumped with excitement, she rushed to the

closet, flipped one-by-one through her clothes, and chose a white dress with ruffles along its scooped neckline. She pulled the dress over her head and wiggled it down her body. The style hugged her hips and gently flared out around her thighs, spurring a smile and a delicious thought:

Sharon's right. I have been keeping to myself too much.

Walking to the other side of the room, she ran her fingers over the fabric of her dress and glanced in the full-length mirror. She was pleased with what she saw. Since her arrival, she had intensified her exercise program and was rewarded with a body to be proud of. Her complexion was clear, and her blue eyes sparkled. The white ruffles of lace covering her breasts made them look more voluptuous than before.

Grinning, she selected a red belt to accent the curve of her waist, stepped into a pair of matching red high heels, and grabbed the strap to her handbag. She was on her way to brave the dangers of the city and find her first adventure.

Chapter THREE

FIVE GREY TANKS CLATTERED over asphalt as they maneuvered past the volleyball court toward the Andrews and McNair Barracks motor pool. Army tanks were as commonplace as cars in the American sector of Berlin, and hardly anyone gave them a glance as they rumbled through the streets. The disturbance only temporarily interrupted the game, then:

Thump.

The volleyball sailed high over the net. Sunlight blinded the receiving team. They crashed into each other as they dived for the ball. It hit the sand.

Several women along the sidelines groaned. They admired the group of handsome men who wore nothing but sunglasses and shorts.

"No fair," Sally yelled, a brunette with enough cleavage to hide the Titanic. "The sun was in their eyes. Interference."

Jake flashed her a rakish smile and laughed. "Ah, Sally, the gods are on our side today. You're rooting for the wrong team. They don't have a prayer of winning."

Thump.

He spun around just in time to leap and spike the oncoming ball. It slammed once more into the sand at the opponents' feet.

Sally turned to her blonde friend and motioned toward Jake with a polished fingernail. "I'd give anything to marry that guy and have his babies."

The blonde smirked. "Good luck with that. Jake's not the marrying type. He doesn't even date."

Not to be dissuaded, Sally licked her lips, returned her gaze to the game, and intensified her mental gun sights on Jake. "I bet you I could win him over," she said, feeling confident in her assets. She adjusted her bikini top with both hands so that her breasts were pushed up higher. "What man could resist these puppies?"

The blonde rolled her eyes. "Don't bite off more than you can chew, girlfriend. He's a heartbreaker."

Jake saw the volleyball spinning toward him. He crouched and yelled, "Set."

"Got it," his best bud, Doug Hanson, called from behind him.

Jake received the full force of the volleyball and bumped it to Doug. He hit it high in the air above Jake's head. Jake waited for the ball to come down, and then at the last second, he slammed the ball over the net for the kill, scoring the final victory point for his team.

As the onlookers leaped up and down cheering for their team, Sally was determined to prove her girlfriend wrong. Jake was an incredibly sexy man with a strong body. How could he possibly resist an evening interlude with her?

Approaching the men, Sally leered at Jake and

Doug, both sweating and breathing hard as they picked up their shirts from the sidelines and used them to wipe their brows. Before long, Jake would be putty in her hands.

The men grabbed a couple sodas from an ice chest and plopped onto the grass alongside the sandy court. Doug was the first to spy Sally bouncing in their direction. "Here comes trouble."

Jake sat with his arms resting on bent knees. Following Doug's gaze, he rolled his eyes and groaned. "I expected Sally to come over here." He raked a hand through his sweat-soaked hair. "She's been checking me out for weeks."

Flashing her prettiest smile, Sally swayed her hips as she sauntered near the two men, hoping that Jake would notice her barely contained breasts within her pink bikini top.

Jake noticed, as did Doug, and both looked down at their feet, trying to restrain their laughter at her blatant boldness.

Sally didn't notice their amusement because she was on a mission. "Oh, Jake," she swooned and struck a sexy pose. "You play volleyball so well." Then breathlessly she asked with a wink, "Do you do everything else equally as well?"

Jake, lifting his head to get a better look at her, shaded his eyes from the afternoon sun. He smiled at her stupid pickup line. She was the last thing he wanted to date, besides, she would have better luck enticing a eunuch.

Interpreting his gaze as an indication of interest,

Sally fluttered her long dark eyelashes and touched her lower lip with a polished fingernail. "Jake, I was wondering, would you like me to cook dinner for you this evening...at my place?" She stared at him, smiling as she mentally sent him this message: *You want me. You really want me now.*

Doug hacked, turned to Jake, and said through feigned coughs, "Hey, buddy, I got to see a man about a horse. You're on your own now." He rushed off toward the barracks. Once inside, he spun around to watch Jake and Sally through the open doorway. Sally was parading back and forth in front of Jake.

Doug burst into laughter. *God, she looks like a cat in heat.*

As she chattered and posed, Sally shook her head, causing her long brown hair to flutter about her bare shoulders.

It was a nice show. Doug eyed her every movement. He admired her long, tan legs. Her shorts were so short that her exposed butt cheeks made him smile with delight. His eyes slowly moved up along her waist to her tie-top bikini. Her breasts were so large that he thought they might escape at any moment. He groaned, thinking that Jake was going to have a great evening with that piece of tail. And why wouldn't he jump at the chance to enjoy this juicy morsel so freely offered in front of his nose? But when Jake shook his head, and Sally's expression turned glum with rejection, Doug lowered his head in disbelief.

Jake was gay. He had to be.

Within moments, Jake strolled into the barracks, chuckling to himself, while Sally pouted and flounced off in a huff toward her laughing girlfriend.

"Have you lost your mind?" Doug punched Jake on the shoulder. "She wanted you, man."

Jake pretended shock. "All German women want American men." Then tossing a glance in Sally's direction, he added, "Besides, I'm not interested in anyone right now, especially someone who has slept with practically every officer in this unit."

Doug shook his head. If she were after him, there would be no hesitation on his part. He imagined her naked body under his, her fingernails clawing at his back while he... He gulped. *Better just let it go.* "Hey, Jake, wanna grab a beer or two?"

"You bet, after I go home and get out of these sweaty clothes." Glancing at his watch, he added, "Meet you in an hour, across the street from my apartment, at Mulino's."

"Great. See you there." Doug loped upstairs toward his room in anticipation of a quick cat-nap, which would energize him for a fun-filled evening of girl-chasing and carousing.

***

Mulino's was a small, locally-owned Italian restaurant across from Andrews Base. It was a favorite American hangout. Plus the food was great. The place was crowded and busy and noisy as usual. Jake leaned back in his chair by the window and took a long drink of his dark German beer while watching the parade of soldiers strolling in and out of the establishment. Most were in their camouflage Battle Dress Uniforms. Others were off duty in civilian clothes. Lieutenant Doug Hanson was easy to spot as he walked in. His powerfully built frame towered above most people. Women considered Doug very good looking—an eight out of ten he'd been told by his gal pals.

Jake waved to get Doug's attention, and then twisted around to call over a waitress. Doug nudged his way through the crowd and pulled up a chair at the table. When the tall and perky waitress approached, Doug ordered a draft beer while his eyes glided over her skimpy bar-maid's dress. She smiled and hurried back through the crowd to get his drink.

"She's a hottie." Doug chuckled. "I bet you I can get her phone number when she returns with my beer."

Jake shook his head and looked across the table at his friend. "Doesn't it get old after a while?"

Doug adjusted his chair closer to the table, frowned a little, and then cleared his throat. "What do you mean?"

Jake's eyes felt heavy. "Have you ever been in love?"

"Every weekend." Doug chortled and slapped the table with his big hand.

"No, seriously." Jake shook off a gnawing sense of concern for Doug's risqué mood. After all, he was young, strong, and had everything to look forward to in life.

The Berlin Affair

Doug leaned toward Jake. "I don't want to settle down with one woman. I want to travel the world and savor every bit of life's flavors."

The waitress returned to their table with his beer on her tray. As she placed the mug down in front of him, he thanked her and tossed a couple of German coins on her tray, and then she moved to another table.

Bringing the beer mug to his lips, Doug took a long noisy slurp and then belched long and hard, as if for comic effect. He patted his stomach then raised his eyebrows at Jake's admonishing look. "Oh, come off it, Jake. You're acting like an old fogy. Lighten up. Besides, your lousy mood distracted me, and I forget to get that waitress's phone number."

Jake guzzled half the beer in his mug. He knew the root cause for his lousy mood.

And good old Doug picked up on it. Settling back into his chair, he said, "It's that old girlfriend of yours, isn't it?" He cocked his big head to one side and arched his brows. "What's her name? Oh yeah. Marianne. That's the one. Right?"

At the sound of her name, Jake's jaw tightened. He gulped the remaining beer in his mug to drown the not-so-pleasant memories that washed over him like tidal waves crashing against the shore.

Doug prodded, "Wanna talk about it?"

"What good would it do?"

"You need to man up and get over whatever it is that's eating at you."

"I don't want to talk about it," Jake spat, and

then held up his empty mug to the waitress. "Another beer please."

Doug eyed Jake until she arrived with his drink. Beating him to the punch, Doug paid the waitress. "Keep the change."

"*Danke*," she said and walked away.

This time Doug didn't lust after her. He took a long draw from his beer while Jake did the same. Jake didn't drink fast because he was thirsty, but because he was pissed off. Doug knew better than to pry, but he did anyway. "Have you ever talked to anybody about what went on between you two?"

"Nope."

Doug came at him from another angle. "Why can't you get that woman out of your system? Maybe if you dated other women, you'd find someone better. Sally would do you in a heartbeat. Might do you some good. Get over being dumped."

Jake flashed his eyes at Doug. "Sally's not worth the sweat, and by the way, Marianne didn't break it off. I did."

"Okay, okay, truce." Doug held up his hands as if they could shield him from Jake's snarl. "I'm your best bud..." he paused long enough to take a swig of beer, "At least I *thought* I was your best bud." He reached across the table and placed his massive hand on Jake's shoulder. "If you can't talk to me, who can you talk to about this?"

Jake glanced at Doug and realized that this over-grown kid just wanted to help him. "I'm sorry for jumping on you like that, but I really don't know what to say. It isn't a pretty story. Maybe some other time, okay?"

Doug squeezed Jake's shoulder. "Anytime you're ready, man, I'm all ears." He flagged the waitress down for another beer.

There wasn't enough beer in the world to help Jake forget what he'd done to Marianne, but that wouldn't stop him from trying. "Another one for me too."

Chapter FOUR

MARIANNE FELT EMPOWERED. Getting around on the subway wasn't as difficult as she imagined. Tall signs with the German words *U-BAHN* (Untergrund Bahnhof) in blue letters made the subway entrances easy to spot on any crowded street. And now, traveling on this massive intra-city rail system, she stared in amazement at the extent of public transportation. No wonder her new employer had told her she didn't need a car in Berlin.

At each stop, subway cars filled with people of all shapes and sizes. She had settled down on one of the bench seats near the sliding doors and clutched her small handbag in her lap. This was her first time on a subway, and she wasn't sure how safe she would be. She didn't want to take any chances with someone snatching her purse.

The car jostled and squealed as it wound around curves in the subway tunnel. Overhead lights flickered, but no one seemed alarmed. Passengers looked as relaxed as if they were sitting in their own living rooms.

At the next station, the train hissed and glided to a stop. The glass doors squeaked open. More passengers poured in and others departed. Marianne glanced above the door at the subway map mounted near the ceiling and noted that she had five more stops to go. She glanced at the passengers entering the train.

Plenty of time to people-watch.

A group of elderly ladies sporting a variety of feather-adorned hats squawked like fat parrots as they nudged each other onto the subway car. Once seated, they huddled together on a bench, each with bundles of daisies decorated with strands of curled ribbon.

A plump woman, at least seventy years old, plopped down on the bench opposite Marianne. The woman's weathered face crinkled into a frown while she reached for something in her over-sized handbag. After a few seconds, she smiled when she revealed what she was reaching for, a fluffy Yorkshire puppy, which poked its tiny head out of the bag and lapped at her owner's hand. The woman smiled at Marianne and lifted the dog from her purse. "I go everywhere with my Heidi," she said in German then placed the wriggling Yorkie on her generous lap.

"What a pretty puppy," Marianne responded in German. She reached across the aisle and scratched Heidi's head. "She's absolutely adorable."

"You're American, are you not?" The woman adjusted her eyeglasses as if she wanted a better view of Marianne. "I can tell by your accent."

"I'm from San Diego. My name is Marianne. What's yours?"

With a wide grin, the woman said, "Ingrid. My name is Ingrid Weinstraub." She cocked her head and added, "Are you new to Berlin?"

"In fact, I am," Marianne replied with a grin. "I've only been here a short time, and this is the first opportunity I've had to explore the city."

This became an invitation for Ingrid to spend the rest of Marianne's subway time telling her about Berlin: the best places to eat, shop, dance, and find young men. Marianne politely nodded her head and interjected a few comments when she could get them in, but she was most amazed at the woman's vocal stamina.

All at once the train lurched around a sharp curve, throwing Marianne off balance and forcing her to grip a nearby handrail. "That was rough." Settling back, she noticed a tall young man standing in the aisle on her left, his right elbow hooked around a metal pole.

Although his back was to her, his tight faded jeans and his colorfully decorated shirt aroused her interest. If only he would turn around so she could get a look at his face. As if on cue, he turned around, and she could hardly keep from laughing. His hair, a rich dark brown from the back, was bleached white in the front, heavily moussed, and shaped to form a four-inch point in front of his face. It looked like a bird's beak.

What a strange fellow.

Ingrid scowled at the man. "The young these days. I don't know what's gotten into their heads." At that, she seemed to forget all about Marianne and began chattering to Heidi. "Children don't have respect, do they, baby."

Heidi squirmed in her lap, tail wagging.

Trying to keep her mind off the comical scene, Marianne decided to check out the other passengers. At the far end of the compartment, a young boy's head bobbed in rhythm to a song on his portable music player. Others seemed content to stare out the window as the city flew by.

The trained slowed down and squeaked to a stop at Wittenbergplatz, Berlin's downtown area. Marianne felt disappointed that she and Ingrid had to part ways.

"*Auf Wiedersehen*," Marianne called out to Ingrid and stepped out of the subway car and onto the platform. Ingrid smiled from her seat and waved behind the window glass as the doors closed.

As soon as she exited the subway station, Marianne's senses were assailed by a myriad of wonderful sights and smells. A little ways down the boulevard stood the tall ruins of the Kaiser Wilhelm Memorial Church, a famous landmark. She opened her travel guide, which explained that the original church on the site was built in the 1890s and was damaged in a 1943 bombing raid. Fortunately, the old church's beautiful spire remained intact.

Shielding her eyes from the sun, she looked up toward the top of the church. A gigantic clock clung to the side of the stone building. The enormous hands could be seen from blocks away.

The bell tower chimed twelve times. Marianne had not yet had her lunch, and the wonderful smell of grilled Bratwurst in the air was too tempting to resist. At first, she couldn't determine where the rich aroma originated, so she followed her nose and spied a small vendor on the other side of the boulevard.

Since her arrival, Marianne had fallen in love with all kinds of German cooking. And the idea of enjoying a Bratwurst cradled in a hard roll and smothered with mustard... well, she dashed across the street toward the little *Imbiss* fast food stand. Many people were already enjoying their lunch, and she noticed they were eating not only Bratwurst, but Weiner Schnitzels, spiced roasted chicken, and French fries.

"Ein Bratwurst, bitte." Marianne held up one finger then pointed to the sizzling sausage.

A heavy-set man wearing a rumpled Led Zeppelin T-shirt and baggy trousers peered up at her from behind the smoky grill. Flashing a wide smile, he selected a plump sausage and placed it in a roll, handed it to her, and winked. "Seven Deutschmark, fraulein."

She pulled out seven coins from her pocketbook and placed them into his meaty hand.

"Danke."

Then she strolled down the street while eating her lunch.

I'm definitely going to like it here.

As she walked along, she admired window displays in an endless row of department stores. Each one competed with the others. Mannequins glittered with the latest fashions from France, Italy, and beyond. She remembered how her friends at work had raved about this one store in particular: the *Kaufhaus Des Westens*, which was the largest department store on the European continent. The sheer height of the store amazed her, and she admired the international flags waving along the building's rooftop. So this was what the locals called the famous *KaDeWe*.

Finished with her lunch, she thought it would be fun to go inside, perhaps check out their shoe department, but when she stepped up to the front door, a metal gate barred the doorway, signifying that the store was closed. Asking a passerby why this would be so, she was told that on Saturdays all stores close at 1pm and would not open again until Monday morning. Maybe it was for the better. She needed to watch her budget because she still had a lot of moving expenses to wrap up. But that wouldn't stop her from looking.

The afternoon flew by as she explored store after store, marveling at all the European fashions displayed in the windows. A rolling rumble of thunder in the distance alerted her that the weather was quickly changing. She looked up and noticed the sky had turned a dark shade of gray. Suddenly, a strange prickly feeling climbed up her spine, alerting her that she was being watched. Goose bumps rose on the back of her neck. She whirled around, only to see people walking up and down the street.

She remembered her security briefing at the Consulate upon her arrival. Although West Berlin was a fairly safe place to live, it was filled with intelligence agents from many countries who might try to get information from an unsuspecting American. It was common for East German or Russian spies to befriend Americans, gather intelligence, and then blackmail them for national security secrets. Because of her unique position at the Consulate, she could be a target for espionage.

She shivered at the thought of a stranger following her.

A flash of lightning forked through the gray sky, sending an ear-splitting crack of thunder and a sudden downpour of cold rain on downtown Berlin. Looking up into the dark clouds, she cursed herself for not bringing her umbrella. She was learning about Berlin's fickle weather the hard way, by getting soaked to the bone. Running down the sidewalk with her hands over her head, she dashed into a bakery doorway and bumped into a man standing there. "Oh, I'm so sorry," she blurted out then gasped, thinking this could be a spy in pursuit of her.

"No. Pardon me, madam." The man's voice, deep and rich, didn't sound menacing. And he spoke perfect English. He wore a silk shirt over his broad chest. Cowering, she glanced up at his face and smiled with the realization that he was tall and handsome.

"I see that you've been caught without your umbrella." The German's smooth voice was filled with humor. "Early Spring always has surprise rain showers."

Marianne gazed into his amused green eyes set in a round, friendly face. He looked too old to be a spy, although she couldn't rule out the fact that there were probably old spies lurking about. This one appeared to be around fifty years old, due to the silver streaks in his hair. And apparently he was on his way out of the bakery with a bag of bread when the rainstorm began. "I don't see your umbrella."

"I too forgot mine." He motioned with a wave of his free hand. "Maybe we should wait here until the rain stops." A smile crinkled the corners of his mouth.

The sky grew darker, and another flash of lightning and crack of thunder made Marianne jump. Then the rain poured harder than before, in thick, gray sheets. "I agree." She shivered and glanced down at her soggy dress, now clinging to her body like she had been in a wet t-shirt contest. "But as soon as it stops, I need a serious cup of coffee."

"I'd be happy to show you a nice café."

"That'll be great."

"Then let me introduce myself. My name is Heinrich." He offered his hand. "What's your name?"

"Marianne Tucker." She accepted his handshake and noticed no rings on either hand.

"And you are an American, I bet."

His warm hand made her feel at ease. "Yes, from California."

They huddled together in the bakery doorway and chatted as they watched the rain and lightning show. His funny stories made her laugh. He told her he was a freelance writer, wrote poems, traveled the world, played guitar, sang in the church choir, and rode Harley Davidson motorcycles. Heinrich had an insatiable thirst for life.

Peering out the doorway toward the sky, he stated, "There now, the rain is beginning to stop." He stepped onto the sidewalk and held out his hand as if to prove his observation. "See, no raindrops."

She laughed. "I'm an American. I'm not blind."

He pointed to a nearby taxi stand. "Are you still interested in getting that coffee you mentioned?"

What a nice gentleman.

"Of course." Her earlier concern about the pursuing spy vanished as quickly as the passing rainstorm.

"Join me in a cab ride?"

"I'd love to." Eager to make new friends, she grinned and held out her arm to be escorted properly. They marched to a waiting taxi. Heinrich opened her door and waited for her to get in. She hesitated for a moment, having second thoughts about whether or not this was a good idea. After all, she didn't know this man, and yet here she was, stepping into a taxi with a stranger to be driven to a place she'd never been before. For all she knew, he could be taking her to a communist detention center where he'd tie her to a chair under a cone of light and beat her until she talked. Well, it could happen...in the movies.

She shook those silly thoughts out of her head, slid into the seat, and chuckled at her wild imagination. "Are you joining me?" she asked Heinrich.

He smiled and then slid in after her.

Too bad he wasn't a spy. He'd have been a good one...in the movies.

***

The German café called a *Konditori* was warm and cozy. Marianne felt she and Heinrich were becoming fast friends. She liked him as a friend, of course, and enthusiastically filled him in on her recent arrival and first impressions of Berlin. Her window shopping activities made her realize how hungry she was. An early supper was definitely what she needed.

"Heinrich." She sighed, motioning to her bowl of hearty vegetable soup. "This is simply wonderful."

"Wait until you try the chicken pastette." He kissed his fingertips. "It will melt in your mouth." He seemed to enjoy watching his new American friend going wild over the native cuisine. She noticed that his gaze wandered over her face and lingered on her lips. He'd better not get any romantic notions. She hoped he'd be comfortable with the fact that they would only be friends.

The chicken pastette did not disappoint her. She closed her eyes and moaned in ecstasy with each exquisite mouthful. And the best thing of all, the prices were reasonable.

She scanned the room. Sprinkled throughout the café, elderly men and women sporting knit or felt hats sat together, eating and chatting. The wait staff didn't try to hurry anyone with their meals or bring the check prematurely in an attempt to shoo them out the door and replace them with fresh-paying customers. Everyone could stay as long as they wanted. Nearby, a woman sat alone and sipped tea while gazing out the window at people walking past. Marianne would bet they all had interesting stories to tell about their lives in Berlin.

Thinking of her subway companion, Ingrid, Marianne smiled. "Since I'm going to be here for a few years, I'd like to get to know the people and this city better."

"Marianne, I will be glad to show you around Berlin, but first, you must taste Berlin."

Wondering what he was referring to, she watched him get up and walk into an adjacent room. He returned, chuckling. "I hope you are not on a diet."

He had hardly finished speaking when a waitress approached the table. She carried two plates of the most decadent chocolate dessert Marianne had ever seen. It had several layers of rich dark chocolate cake with alternating layers of white Bavarian cream dotted with black cherries. The waitress placed the dishes and silverware in front of them, gave Heinrich a knowing smile, and hustled back to the kitchen.

Marianne's mouth hung wide open in amazement. She looked at Heinrich, who was laughing, and then returned her eyes to the dessert. "I've gained ten pounds just looking at it."

"Genuine Black Forest cake, Marianne. It will turn you into a true Berliner." Heinrich laughed and added, "Do you know a famous American who said he was a *Berliner*?"

"No, please tell me."

"In 1963, your President John F. Kennedy stood in front of the people of Berlin and said these famous words, *Ich bin ein Berliner*. I am a Berliner." Heinrich's eyes twinkled. "You will be in good company."

Marianne laughed.

Heinrich tipped his head in the direction of her dessert. "You have not touched your cake. Does it not look good to you?"

"It looks too good to eat."

He placed a fork in her hand. "Eat. There are plenty of other things you'll want to experience."

She stabbed her fork into the sumptuous chocolate and soon felt as if she would float away to heaven.

"That's good, eh?"

She nodded and cleaned her plate. If she had been alone, she would have licked it.

Heinrich motioned to the waitress for the check.

"Heinrich, please let me pay for my portion."

"Nothing of the sort. You are my guest." Taking her hand, Heinrich said, "Come, Marianne. Let's go for a walk. I want to show you my Berlin."

This time she flinched at the touch of his hand. It was warm and comforting, but a little overly familiar. Emotions conflicted within her. On one hand, she felt some attraction toward Heinrich. He was handsome, worldly, and very much a gentleman. On the other hand, what was he expecting from her in return for the meal and the tour? His attentiveness toward her indicated romantic interest, yet for all she knew, she could be misinterpreting his actions altogether. She took a deep breath, smiled, and squeezed his hand. She wanted to experience her new adventure, and it seemed the universe was more than happy to deliver it to her.

Problem was, could she handle it? Was she emotionally ready for what the universe had in mind?

Chapter FIVE

MONDAY MORNING, the Operations office phones were ringing off the hook. Jake tried unsuccessfully to tune them out as he wandered among the myriad of busy workers at their desks. They looked very much like ants gathering papers and files and moving them from one location to another, and then back again. Massaging his aching neck, he surveyed the chaotic scene. The press would have a field day if this news got out. Good thing everyone in this room was sworn to secrecy.

The Army was a big change from the civilian jobs he'd held before. From finance accountant and mortgage broker to military protocol and international negotiations, he now worked with MI (Military Intelligence) under the direction of *The Major*. Jake was actually a glorified secretary, of sorts, handling the paperwork and media releases for all of Western Europe. Negotiations with Günter Schabowski of East Germany over the future of the Berlin Wall had taken up most of the department's time lately.

He glanced at the reception area outside of the adjacent finance department and watched the long line of soldiers patiently waiting to get inside, each with a *life-threatening* problem, hoping that their dilemmas would allow them to be seen first. It would be a long night for those boys. Jake glanced at his watch. Almost time for his duty shift to end. Satisfied his team was on schedule, he walked back into his office.

"Hey there, best bud, you look beat."

Jake jumped at the unexpected voice and saw Lieutenant Doug Hanson sitting in a chair propped back on two legs against the wall. "What are you doing here?" He stepped behind his desk and slumped into his leather chair.

"Little jumpy, aren't we?"

"I'm bushed." Jake picked up a pen off his desk and muttered, "I haven't been able to get much rest lately."

"Think fast." Doug tossed him a rectangular-shaped box.

Jake caught it. The weight surprised him, and he almost dropped it. "What the hell?"

"Open it."

Jake tossed Doug the pen. "What's in here?"

"I got you a little something."

Jake opened the box and lifted out a marble nameplate. On the smooth top, the irregular shape of Berlin had been inlaid in cloisonné art. The city was colorfully divided into the four sectors: French, British, American, and Soviet. The front-side of the nameplate gleamed with shiny brass letters:

1st Lieutenant Jake Adams

"Well, do you like it?"

"Yeah, this is great."

"How does it feel to be newly promoted?"

"I don't know yet." Jake grinned as he pushed aside a tower of paperwork and positioned the nameplate on the front of his desk. "Does the promotion come with an easier job?"

"I'll let you know when I get promoted." Doug laughed.

"I've only been on this Berlin Solution assignment a couple of months, and already this place is driving me crazy. Keeps me up half the night."

"I'm disappointed in you." Doug twirled the pen around his meaty fingers. "I hoped the reason you weren't getting enough sleep was due to some delightful female's companionship."

Jake rocked back in his chair. The only female he was interested in got away. Glancing sideways, he motioned with a tilt of his head toward the stacks of paper so high that the desk underneath was impossible to see. "That's my new girlfriend. And she is very demanding."

Doug glanced at the papers and shuddered. "Way too much work for one person. Let's get out of here and grab a brew."

"I'll meet you at Mulino's right after duty shift change. We'll grab some chow too."

Leaping to his feet, Doug saluted. "Be my pleasure, Sir."

Jake returned the salute though he knew Doug was just horsing around. "That will be all, Lieutenant. Dismissed."

Doug swiveled about and marched out, his head

barely clearing the top door jam.

Jake watched him go then stroked the smooth surface of his new nameplate. What good was a promotion without someone to share it with? Life's experiences seemed to hold little meaning. Though he was working with the Major on a history-making deal that would shock the world, all he really wanted was to go back and change the past.

***

Mulino's was not crowded, much to Jake's relief. As he relaxed into the chair's back cushion, he worked on a heady glass of Berliner Bier. Doug, sitting across from him, eyed the waitress.

"She's married," Jake barked. "Don't get any bright ideas."

Doug frowned. "Hey, what's up with you, man? I was just looking."

Maybe deep down Jake was a little envious of his best bud, free of heart, free of mind, not burdened with memories of a lost love. "I'm bummed, Marianne and all."

"Well, don't take it out on me. I drink to have fun. You just drink and mope."

"Your entire life is a party, Doug. Not everyone is as happy as you."

"Lighten up. If you're just going to bring me down, I'll drink somewhere else."

"You'd just walk out?"

"In a heartbeat. You can drink alone until you're ready to rejoin the human race."

"I can't help it. I miss her."

Doug stood. "Cry in your beer all you want. I hope she's worth it."

"Sit down." Jake didn't want to drink alone. Doug deserved an explanation. Now was as good a time as any. "You want to hear the story?" He paused to swallow the lump in his throat. "I'll tell you what happened, but I don't know where to start."

Doug retook his seat and leaned forward. "Try the beginning."

Jake's stomach fluttered, and he took a large gulp of his beer. Both negative and positive memories swirled in his mind. "It's complicated."

"Where did you meet her?"

Jake made the leap. "After getting my business degree at California State University Fullerton, I accepted a financial management job in San Diego. While there, I attended a computer conference, and that's where I met Marianne."

"I know. It was love at first sight."

Jake looked directly into Doug's eyes. "There is such a thing, you know, and it lasts more than one night."

"We're not talking about my love life, we're talking about yours."

Jake cleared his throat. "We dated seriously for a year and got engaged. That was the best year of my life."

"So what did you do to screw it up?"

Jake shook his head. "I got thrown in jail."

Doug winced. "What the hell did you do

wrong?"

"Nothing."

"Yeah right. They don't throw people in jail for nothing."

Jake swirled the dregs of his beer around in his glass. He had shared his arrest record with the security officer who had conducted Jake's background check for his clearance, so it wasn't a secret, but he didn't want to share his dirty laundry with just anyone. But Doug was different. He really was his best bud.

"Keep this between you and me, you hear?"

"Scouts honor." Doug held up the two finger pledge.

The waitress interrupted them. "Two more for you guys?"

Jake swallowed. "Sure, another round. It's on him." He pointed to Doug.

Doug didn't even flinch. "So what happened?"

"I was framed, lost every dime I owned, and was stuck in jail because I couldn't post bond."

"Wow. Framed for what? Who framed you?"

Jake clenched his jaw. *Embezzlement and that bitch...* He couldn't even say her name. Hurt his brain to even think it. *Sylvia.* "What does it matter? In the end, I lost Marianne."

"Humph," Doug muttered, studying his beer. "I lost my car keys once, found 'em, though."

"When I got out of jail, I tried to find her, but her phone was disconnected, she'd moved out of our apartment, and I heard that she had found someone else."

"Because you got thrown in jail?"

"She didn't even know about that."

"Then what the hell did you do to piss her off?"

A heavy-set waiter waddled up to their table and took their dinner orders, Chicken Parmesan for Doug, Spaghetti for Jake. Extra garlic bread. Once the waiter left, Jake lowered his voice, glanced to the right and left, and then felt a little silly for even thinking that anyone nearby would be interested in or even care what he was about to say. "I left her standing at the altar."

"You're shittin' me."

"I was AWOL on our wedding day."

"Cold feet?"

"I was in jail. Have you been listening?"

Doug took a slug of beer. "Go back the part about why you were in jail."

"To understand that, I have to tell you something first. I had a girlfriend, a pretty serious one before I met Marianne."

Doug's brows shot up in surprise. "Ah-ha. The plot thickens. Who was she?"

Scowling at the curvy image forming in his mind, Jake spat out her name. "Sylvia."

There. He'd said it. It's finally out like a decayed tooth had been yanked from his jaw.

"Good looking?"

He *would* ask that. "Yeah, dynamite." Jake was feeling more at ease; he could breathe. His heart grew a coat of armor as he rolled her name over his tongue again. "Sylvia was a *very* sexy Accounts Manager at the investment firm where I was working before all the nasty stuff happened."

The waitress brought two beers. Doug paid. "What nasty stuff?" The waitress gave him a funny look. He waved her off.

Jake shifted in his seat. "In the course of business, I saw a lot of her, and one thing led to another, and we hit it off. She was a vixen in the rack, but after a while I had second thoughts about her. Demanding. High maintenance. We fought all the time. Power struggle, you know the type. Buy me this, buy me that. My wallet had its own revolving door. Money money money. Turns out she was a real bitch."

"Then you met Marianne, huh?"

"I asked her out knowing full well I'd have to break it off with Silvia."

Doug harrumphed. "The honorable thing to do."

"Don't you get it? I dumped her for Marianne."

"Oh, I see. That made Marianne *the other woman*," he made air quotes, "to Sylvia. Marianne, the homewrecker. Marianne the dream-destroyer. Marianne, the—"

"Okay, so you do understand the position I put her in."

"So how did she feel about being the other woman?"

Jake gulped beer. The truth would set him free. "I didn't tell her."

"Whoa, man. She didn't know about Sylvia?"

"I didn't want her to know that Sylvia was a sore loser. She wouldn't take 'no' from me. She hounded me night and day, trying to get me to break it off with Marianne and marry her instead. Finally I couldn't take it any longer. I just walked away from her. And my last memory of Sylvia was her screaming at me, 'If I can't have you, no one else will either.' I thought I was protecting Marianne from the stress, the headaches, and even the angst."

"Dangerous game, man."

"Sylvia might have gone Postal on Marianne, for all I knew."

Jake had Doug's full attention. This story had the elements of a good thriller like *Fatal Attraction*. "So Sylvia got you thrown in jail?"

"Our wedding was supposed to be on a Saturday afternoon. The night before, we had our rehearsal and dinner. Things were going great. Marianne and I were excited and looking forward to starting our new life together. She spent the night with her parents so that we wouldn't see each other before the wedding." Jake laughed at the memory. "Silly superstition, but it was what she wanted. So on Saturday, just as I was about to leave for the church, that's when the police knocked on my door."

"No way."

"I was arrested for embezzlement." Jake made a fist. "Imagine me, an embezzler. I was hauled to the police station like a common criminal, booked, and wasn't allowed to make a phone call."

"That's not right," Doug grumped. "Everybody

arrested gets one phone call."

"Sylvia had persuaded a couple of her cop buddies to deny me the call until Monday."

"That bitch."

"She always bragged about having friends in high places."

"You sure know how to pick 'em, pal."

"I figured I'd at least be able to post bond the next day and then explain to Marianne what happened, but not only was the bond $500,000, I suddenly discovered that I had no money in my checking or savings accounts."

Doug shook his head in disbelief. "What happened to the money?"

"At that point, I didn't care. I was more worried about Marianne. Even if I was able to contact her, I couldn't imagine trying to explain Sylvia to her."

"So you didn't call her at all?"

"I called my lawyer. I figured I'd beat the rap and set things straight after that, but things went from bad to worse. Because I had no money, my lawyer wouldn't take my case, so I was assigned a public defender, some young rookie who made a ton of mistakes. So I was stuck in jail without bond. That's a nasty position to be in. Fortunately, when the prosecutors put their case together, they came to the conclusion that the evidence against me was too flimsy and wouldn't hold water. So after about six months, the charges were dropped with prejudice, meaning that if new evidence surfaces later, I could be recharged."

Doug whistled. "That must have been hell. All because of one pissed off woman."

"Let that be a lesson to you, my friend."

Doug shook his head, frowning into his empty beer glass. "But you have unfinished business with Marianne. She doesn't know about any of this or that you still love her or if you're dead or alive. That's got to suck."

"All she knows is that I stood her up at the altar."

"You've got to find her, man."

"Why rip the scab off an old wound? Besides, once I tell her about Sylvia, Marianne will be gone anyway."

"And what if she isn't? What if she loves you more than you gave her credit for? Then what?"

"It's better this way."

"For you or for her?"

"For her, of course. It's been hell for me."

"So you run off and join the Army so you don't have to tell her about Sylvia. Sounds like a cop-out to me."

"No, not at all. I couldn't take the chance that Sylvia would come up with some other cockamamie scheme to get me thrown back into jail."

"So you ran."

Jake felt guiltier than ever before. Damn it. He should have manned up, tried harder to find Marianne, and fought Sylvia tooth and nail. He ground his teeth in frustration.

Their food arrived. The waiter placed the dishes

in front of them. "Will there be anything else, gentlemen?"

Doug straightened up. "We're good, thanks." He stabbed a fork into his chicken. "Most guys join for God and country. You joined to get away from a woman. You know how pathetic that sounds?"

Jake eyed his plate of spaghetti and hoped that his nervous stomach would keep it down. "It was the only way I could protect myself. Marianne was long gone. What else did I have to lose?"

Doug shrugged. "Jake, you're an honest guy, and if joining the Army helped you deal with your problem, then who am I to doubt you? It's still pathetic."

"I just wish Marianne and I could be together." He toyed with his food. "I imagine she hates me too much for that to ever happen."

"Why don't you track her down and win her back?"

"Win her back?" Jake's voice cracked with disbelief. His friend was asking the impossible.

"What do you have to lose? Get a hold of Sam Clawson at 766MID. He'll find her." His eyes bored into Jake's as if daring him to take on the challenge. "Those intelligence boys can find anybody."

Jake shook his head. His mouth went dry. "It would never work between us. Even if Sam found her for me, she'd sooner see me dead than take me back. I abandoned her. She'd never forgive me."

"Listen, you idiot." Doug's voice started to rise in volume as if he was tired of Jake's reluctance to redeem himself. "So what if you were a stupid jerk and lied to Marianne?"

"I didn't lie to her."

"You didn't tell her about Sylvia."

"That's not lying."

"A lie by omission is still a lie," he shouted. "She deserved to know about Sylvia. You made a mistake, but what really takes the cake is that you're not trying to rectify that mistake."

Jake glanced around to see if anyone had noticed Doug's loud voice. "Come on now, calm down—"

"No, I won't calm down." Doug pounded his fist on the table. "You're lucky. I *never* felt that strongly about *any* woman, and if I did, I wouldn't sit around feeling sorry for myself. I'd hire an investigator or do whatever was necessary to find her and tell her everything that happened. If she forgave me, then great, if not, at least I could say I tried. I'd get her out of my system once and for all and move on with my life."

Jake stared in mute amazement at Doug, the womanizer who would never settle down, but now Jake was shocked to learn how deeply Doug felt about love. It touched him to the core. "You're just a softie."

"You're still an idiot."

Feeling a sense of doom, Jake considered his friend's challenge. Perhaps there was still a chance to regain what he had lost. No matter how the search ended, he'd have some resolution on the matter. And so would Marianne. "You know, you're right. All she can do is say no..."

"Now you're talking. Let's order dessert."

"...or shoot me."

***

Be it known that Sam Clawson, having served behind the Iron Curtain and having combated the threat of hostile intelligence in the free city of West Berlin is this date designated a Silent Warrior...

"Like my plaque?"

Jake whirled around and grinned at the agent who had stepped up behind him. "Yes. It's very cool." He'd been standing in the waiting room at 766MID. "I like the picture of the Brandenburg Gate on the aged parchment. I'm Jake, by the way." He offered a handshake.

Sam smiled and shook Jake's hand. "I know who you are." Sam was in his late forties, retired Army, and according to his own account, he didn't feel compelled to relax his military appearance. He preferred to keep in shape and maintain his hair in a standard butch crew-cut.

"What did you find out?"

"I did a quick background check on you. Looks like you had a fun time with the legal system a while back."

Jake's jaw twitched. "Unfortunately yes, but that was cleared up, well, for the most part."

"Charges were dismissed with prejudice. Kinda like walking around with an anvil over your head, don't you think? Could drop at any time."

"Someday I hope to prove my innocence."

Sam nodded. "Doug said you needed some help finding Marianne Tucker."

"I do. I think she still lives in San Diego. Would you be interested in doing some moonlight investigative work for me?"

Sam pursed his lips as if considering the challenge. "766 Military Intelligence Detachment is the premier counter-intelligence detachment of the Army. We have our thumb firmly on the pulse of Berlin. Nobody sneezes without somebody around here knowing about it."

"The sales pitch really isn't necessary."

"I know, but you liked my plaque."

Jake rolled his eyes. "What about Marianne Tucker?"

"Doug Hanson already gave us the target."

"She's my fiancé, not a target."

"Ex-fiancé from what I understand."

"It's complicated."

"So I've heard. I'll just call her a target. Keeps the job less personal for me, you know."

These intelligence guys were whacko. "So did you find her?"

Sam picked up a phone on the desk, punched a number, and handed Jake the receiver. "Not exactly."

The phone rang in Jake's ear. If Marianne were to pick up, what would he say?

Sam said, "It's her cousin, Sharon."

"Hello," came over the line.

Jake's throat tightened. He couldn't get a word

out.

"Anybody there?"

He had to say something or she'd hang up. "Sharon?"

"Yes?"

"It's Jake."

Silence.

"Hello?"

"You low down slimy—"

"I need to speak with Marianne." His heart was beating so loud he thought surely she'd hear it in San Diego. "Do you know where she is?"

"She's...not...here."

"I know you're mad—"

"Mad? You don't know what mad is, mister."

"Look—"

"No, you look, Jake. I wouldn't tell you where she is if you were the last man on earth. Got that?"

"I have to explain to her what happened."

"She doesn't care anymore, you bastard."

"Give me a chance—"

"She left a message for me to give you, just in case you crawled out from under a rock someday."

"A message, all right, what is it?"

"Go to hell."

Click! The line went dead.

"Damn."

Sam held out his hand for the phone. "Didn't go so good, huh?"

"She hates me."

"Can you blame her, really?"

"What now?"

"We'll keep looking."

Another agent stepped out of the backroom. Jake guessed that was where they kept all their supercomputers. The agent handed Sam a piece of paper. He looked at it, looked up, and grinned ear to ear.

"What is it?"

"Seems the American Consulate right here in Berlin has a new employee. A Passport Officer."

Confusion racked Jake's brain. "So?"

"Her name is Marianne Tucker."

A dizzy swirl damn near knocked Jake off his feet. He braced himself on the desk. She was in Berlin. There'd be no letters or phone calls needed to confess and beg for forgiveness. He could see her face-to-face. His day of reckoning was closer than he could have ever imagined.

Chapter SIX

THE AMERICAN CONSULATE WAS busier than ever, now that it was early summer. Vacationers from all over Europe flocked to Berlin, the Jewel City of Germany, and some of those travelers were Americans who had questions about their passports or local military families wanting visas to travel to other countries. Marianne was responsible for ensuring the paperwork was in order, along with performing computer background checks as needed.

She finished helping a young military couple complete the necessary paperwork for a visa to Spain. The soldier's wife had talked about their plans to visit Malaga and Gibraltar, and even take a boat trip across to Morocco. When they left on their great adventure, their eagerness and energy remained behind as a warm glow in Marianne's office.

She was sitting at her desk, organizing a small pile of forms, when a woman appeared in the doorway. Beautiful, refined, and with an elegant aura about her, the woman looked like she could have been royalty. She appeared to be in her early thirties. Her beige dress looked custom made because it hugged every curve of her tall, voluptuous frame. Wearing a white wide brimmed hat accented with a long green feather, she reeked of money and entitlement.

"May I help you?"

"I lost my passport."

"Please, come in." Marianne offered her the cushy chair in front of her desk.

The woman sat and uttered an irritated sigh, as if she were put out by being there.

Marianne got down to business. "I'll need to see some identification."

The woman searched through her handbag and produced a leopard-print wallet. "I arrived in Berlin a week ago. Misplaced the damn thing. I need you to make a new one for me right away." She pulled out her identification and a birth certificate then brushed a lock of black hair behind one ear and added, "I have my passport number, if that helps."

Her slim hand displayed an array of diamond rings that accented her long fingernails. She handed the documents to Marianne, who studied them closely then glanced at the woman to compare her face to the picture on her California driver's license. Everything seemed to be in order, and after a background check, it would be easy to issue her a new passport.

"Okay, Mrs. Maderas—"

"Miss," she snapped in a pompous voice. "I'm not married."

"All-righty then, *Miss* Maderas." Marianne placed a form in front of the not-so charming woman. "Please fill this out while I copy your documents. I'll be right back."

She eyed the paper and huffed. "Really?"

"It's an affidavit attesting to how you lost your passport. We need it for our records."

She snarled under her breath and began to fill out the form.

Meanwhile, in the backroom, Marianne copied the documents and filed a stop on the missing passport in case it showed up anywhere in the wrong hands. Returning to her desk, she noted that the woman had completed the form.

Miss Maderas stared at her with dagger-sharp eyes. "What took you so long?"

Marianne felt a twitch in her stomach, unsure how to react to someone so rude, but she persevered in her professional manner. "Your new passport will be ready in a few days." She inspected the form and located the address where Miss Maderas was staying. "When it's ready we'll give you a call and have it delivered to you."

"Why can't I have it now?"

"Sorry. These things take time."

"That's absurd."

"I don't make the rules." She handed the woman her original documents.

The woman's dark eyes narrowed as she snatched them from Marianne's hand. "Fine! I'll wait for your call." She adjusted her hat and then stormed out the door.

Marianne watched the woman strut out of sight. She didn't think she had ever encountered a woman so elegant, so striking, yet her gruff and hostile personality made her an ugly person. She looked at all the paperwork involved in replacing the passport and decided to instruct Carla, her administrative assistant, to handle Miss Maderas's problem.

Marianne didn't want anything more to do with her.

Chapter SEVEN

JAKE STARTED UP the concrete steps to the American Consulate. Pausing mid-step, he glanced at the expensive bouquet of flowers in his hands and questioned himself. *Do I really need to go through with this?*

He scanned the area behind him, the sidewalk, the taxis, the buses, a dozen ways to escape, a dozen reasons to turn around, but one reason to press on: Marianne.

But how would she react to seeing him? Would she cry? Would she scream? Would she slap his face and beat on his chest with clenched fists?

Shut up and man-up, Jake. You can do this.

Whatever her reaction, whatever the outcome, he would deserve every bit of her wrath. Swallowing his fears, he entered the building.

Security stopped him. "Let's see some ID, Lieutenant."

Jake showed his military ID to the guard, who studied it, compared the picture on the card to Jake's face, and then eyed the flowers suspiciously. "What you got in there? A gun. A knife? A Bazooka?"

"Just flowers."

The guard produced a metal detecting wand and waved it over the flowers, up and down and underneath. The device remained mute. "Humph."

"I told you so."

He motioned him into the metal detector.

Jake stepped through it, hoping it wouldn't start beeping. The burly guard looked ready to pounce, like he would enjoy harassing him over a belt buckle or a money clip or a bazooka.

No sounds, no bells, or whistles. Jake was deemed *clean.* A second guard waved him in.

Taking a deep breath to steady his nerves, he stepped up to the information counter. "Excuse me. Would you please direct me to Marianne Tucker's office?"

The Information Specialist eyed Jake and raised his eyebrows when he noticed the bouquet of flowers. "Do you have an appointment?"

"No, I don't but—"

"What's your name? I'll call up and tell her you're here."

"Ah, wait, ah," Jake stammered. He didn't want Marianne to know he was here. She could refuse to see him or duck out the back door, blowing his chance to talk to her. "Look. It's her birthday. I want to surprise her." He indicated the flowers as proof of his intentions. "You wouldn't want to ruin it for her, would you?"

"Nobody ever brings me flowers on my birthday."

"I'll remember next time. What do you say?"

The specialist's eyes sparkled. "Just go up the stairs and through the glass doors on the right. That's the passport office. You'll find her there."

"Thanks...and happy birthday."

"It's in two months. On the twentieth. Don't forget."

Funny guy.

Jake trudged up the stairs to the second floor and easily found the passport office. Pausing outside the main glass doorway, he rehearsed in his mind all the things he wanted...no, needed to say. His heart pounded with trepidation. This could ruin her day. Ruin the rest of his life. But maybe seeing her could be a new beginning for them. Somehow he didn't think that would be so easy.

Taking a deep breath, he pushed the door open and walked in.

Chapter EIGHT

ALMOST BURIED UNDER a pile of computer printouts, Marianne flipped through page after page, searching for the information she would need to finish her status report.

Too much to do in too little time.

While dealing with the mountain of paperwork, she heard growing chatter from her co-workers who were commenting about a man who had entered the passport lobby.

"Army brass. Will you take a look at that guy," one of them whispered.

"He's an Adonis, all right," another said.

"I wonder who the flowers are for," someone else put in.

Marianne wondered what all the commotion was about. The hallway outside her office sounded like the inside of a girl's high school locker room with all the giggling going on. She gathered her stack of papers and carried it out of her office. "What's all the fuss about?" she asked the women huddled in the hallway, just out of view from the lobby.

"Check out the Army hunk." Carla nudged Marianne's elbow. "And he's not wearing a ring." She must've thought matchmaking was part of her administrative assistant duties.

Marianne took a peek for herself. On the other side of the counter stood a man wearing an Army uniform. His back was to her, but she could see the flowers he carried and a silver bar on the shoulder loop of his regulation jacket. He looked to be over six feet tall and chiseled to perfection. Still, there was no call for all this giddiness. "Don't just stand there. Carla, see what he wants."

Carla skipped out to the counter.

"The rest of you, back to work." Marianne ducked into the backroom to use the copy machine. She didn't even have time to set the papers down when she heard Carla greet the officer.

"May I help you, sir?" Her voice was syrupy sweet.

"I'm here to see Marianne Tucker," he said.

Marianne's heart studder-stepped. That voice was like a slap in the face. Sounded just like Jake Adams. Couldn't be.

"I'll get her for you." Carla said it like the wind had been knocked out of her.

Marianne swallowed hard. *What the hell is going on?*

In a heartbeat, Carla was at the backroom door. "It's for you."

"Who is he?"

"He's got flowers, who cares?"

Marianne hugged the papers to her chest and stepped into the lobby. "How can I help you?"

The officer turned to face her. Colorful service ribbons pinned to his broad chest caught her eye first.

Perfectly pressed slacks, polished shoes. She realized she was deliberately avoiding his face.

"Hello, Marianne."

She suddenly felt dizzy at the sound of Jake Adams' voice again. She forced herself to look at him, to confirm the impossible. Handsome chin, smooth cheeks, chestnut eyes, straight nose. Her mind turned to silly putty. What was he doing here? Of all places on earth. How did he find her? Was this some kind of a bad joke? Her heart raced, but her arms felt numb, causing the papers to slip from her grasp and fall to the floor.

Hot fury rose from deep within her core and pulsed in her neck. Jaw clenched, she was speechless with shock.

Jake rushed to her. "Here, let me help you with that." He bent to pick up the papers.

Suddenly embarrassed by her stupid display of emotion, she steeled herself and stooped next to him. "I'll get them." She scrambled about, hands trembling, heart lurching. The last thing she wanted was for Jake to see how he'd affected her.

"Please let me help you." His velvety-smooth voice poured over her senses like melted butter. He offered her the bouquet of flowers. "But you'll have to hold these."

"Seriously?"

"Yes. They're for you."

Marianne stared at him, and then at the flowers. She'd rather beat him senseless with them. But she had a better idea. "Then if they are mine, can I do what I want with them?"

"Of course."

"How sweet of you."

She accepted the flowers, stood, and promptly jammed them upside down in the nearest trash can.

"Marianne, please, I know you're angry, but—"

"Angry?" she screamed. "How about hurt, crushed, devastated, destroyed? Angry is nothing." She shoved him away and dropped to her knees to continue rounding up her papers. "I don't need your help. I don't want your help, and I certainly don't want your stinking flowers."

Everyone in the office was looking at her like she'd lost her mind.

But Jake persisted in collecting the scattered papers. "I'm sorry. I want to explain."

"I don't need your explanations either." She lied. And worse, being this close to him on the floor, his shower-fresh scent made her feel nostalgic for the good times they'd shared together. The times after they'd showered. The times they'd...

Stop it, Marianne. You hate him, don't forget that, not ever.

Both reached for the same document and accidently touched hands. Marianne thought she would explode from the electric sparks surging up her arm and flying through her body. The shock was enough to jolt her back to her senses. "Go away." Her voice took on a steely tone. She pushed his hand back and gathered the rest of the papers in a disheveled wad and stood up to face him.

A couple of concerned coworkers and Carla stepped forward. "Should we call security?"

"I've got this handled." Marianne threw Jake a heated gaze. "He was just leaving."

He responded by scanning her body up and down. "I've missed you."

She felt violated by his blatant assessment and hugged the papers to her chest to block his view of her minimal cleavage. "You have a lot of nerve coming here."

"I have to talk to you." He reached for her arm.

She pulled back. "Don't touch me." She hoped the ice in her voice would freeze him where he stood. How dare he just show up and act as if nothing had happened. Still, every part of her body was thrilled to see him again, and this internal betrayal infuriated and confused her.

Jake smiled. "I want to put us back together again."

"I'm not Humpty Dumpty." She wondered if Jake realized how lame he sounded. What she really wanted to hear was why he'd left her at the altar. And why had he dropped off the face of the earth? There wasn't enough superglue in the word to mend that fence. "I don't want us back together. I don't want to ever see you again." She narrowed her eyes with fury to be sure he got the message.

"Give me another chance. That's all I'm asking."

"You're too late."

He winced.

She saw determination in his eyes, but did he

really think she would be that easy to win back?

How stupid is he?

"Let me take you to lunch today."

Her jaw dropped. He acted like he was in complete control, like this day was no different than any other day. "Lunch? You have got to be kidding." She rolled her eyes in disgust and turned to storm away, but before she could take a step, Jake's strong hand grasped her arm and stopped her.

"Wait, please."

She glared at his hand on her arm. "Let... Go... Of... Me."

"Marianne—"

"Carla, call security."

That didn't stop Jake. "I have to talk to you, explain what happened."

She stared at him. Sure, she had a lot of questions that went unanswered, but she didn't really want to find out what happened. It was water under the bridge. That boat had sailed. The fat lady already sang. Her life was going smoothly again, and she didn't need Jake to upset the apple cart. Clichés were coming at her like hailstones. He'd broken her heart once, shame on him. If he broke it again, shame on her. Now that it was finally mended, or so she'd convinced herself, she wasn't about to throw it under the bus. "I'm busy for the rest of my life." She shrugged off his grip. "Now go away, or I'll have you arrested."

"Come on, Marianne." Jake scratched his chin as if assessing the possibility of the military police hauling him off to jail. "It's just lunch. Please."

She shook her head no, but this time she felt her resolve weakening at the thought of his arms holding her tight against his naked body. She glanced at the floor, and gathering her mental strength, focused on breathing. Her emotions were a jumble, but she held on to her sanity, her dignity, her pride. "And then what? After lunch. You want to hold my hand? Make out? Take me to bed? It's never just lunch." She glared at him and hoped he'd take the hint.

But he didn't budge. Just stood there looking at her with those puppy-dog brown eyes.

Why doesn't he just go away?

"I'll tell you what happened, and then you decide about the other stuff."

"No." She stared straight into his eyes and decided this conversation was over. "Don't waste your breath. I don't know how you found me, but don't ever come back again."

"But Marianne—"

"What don't you understand about *get out*?"

He stepped back and studied her.

Does he think I really didn't mean that?

She glimpsed the hurt flitting in his eyes and immediately felt bad about being so cold. Was she being unfair to him? But Jake had showed her that life wasn't fair. He deserved a taste of his own rejection. She pointed to the door. "Go."

He shrugged. "Some other time, perhaps?"

"Never."

His lower lip quivered then he turned and

walked out.

Marianne's legs crumpled beneath her. As she dropped to the floor, her coworkers rushed to her side. She felt weak, beaten, ruined. Her hands trembled as she accepted a small paper cup of water and brought it to her lips as her coworkers bombarded her with questions.

"What was that all about?"

"Who is he?"

"How could you send such a hunk out of here like that?"

"Give him to me, I'll take him."

Marianne swallowed the water and wished it was poison. She looked over the women gathered around her. They just didn't understand. She rubbed her aching temples in a circular motion with her fingers. The last thing she wanted was to come across as weak, but this was way too much emotional baggage to bear. Some of her coworkers knew about her past, so that helped ease her embarrassment. She pointed to the spot where he had stood. "That...was Jake."

A couple of women moaned. A couple swooned. Most nodded in sympathetic understanding.

Carla knelt to Marianne's eye level. "He'll be back, you know. He doesn't look like the kind of guy who gives up easily. He wants you to forgive him."

Marianne clenched her fists. "I'd rather be hit by a freight train."

***

The next day, a messenger carried a long slender package, topped with a red bow, into the Passport Office. "I'm looking for Marianne Tucker." He glanced around the office filled with women.

"Over there." Several gals pointed in Marianne's direction.

Wondering who would send her a package, she excused herself from the group meeting she was facilitating and strolled toward the courier. "Who is it from?"

"Don't know, ma'am." The messenger grinned as he presented her the package.

"Thank you."

He saluted her, did a sharp about face, and pushed out the glass doors.

Several women gathered around. "Marianne has an admirer," one said. "Who is it?" another asked. "Jake. I'll bet it's from Jake," someone else chimed in.

Marianne tugged at a small envelope attached under the bow. The package was probably from Heinrich. Jake wouldn't be stupid enough to buy more flowers that'd only end up in the trash. Keeping everyone in painful suspense, she opened the flap and withdrew the note.

"It was good to see you yesterday morning," she read aloud. "Love, Jake." The wind left her lungs.

What's he trying to pull?

"I was right. I was right," miss smarty-pants gloated as if she'd won the lottery.

"Wonderful," Carla said. "Open the package."

"Yes, open it," someone else added.

"Let's see what you got," another said and handed her a scissors.

Marianne cut the ribbon and ripped off the wrapping. As she lifted out a long-stemmed red rose in a crystal vase, a chorus of ooohs and aaahs filled the air.

This must have cost Jake plenty.

But she couldn't accept anything from him. There were no doubt strings attached. She shoved it back into the box. "Send this back," she told Carla.

Her coworkers shrugged. Carla said, "You can't be serious." She grabbed the box and removed the vase. "It'll look beautiful on your desk."

"But it'll remind me of Jake. I came to Berlin to forget about him."

Carla broke up the box and tossed it in the trash. Handing the rose and vase back to Marianne, she said, "It needs water."

Marianne inhaled the sweet scent of the rose and grinned at her coworkers' enthusiasm. Forever the matchmakers.

"Okay, everyone, back to work." Marianne shooed them away and walked over to the drinking fountain to pour some water into the vase. It was like putting gasoline on a fire she wanted to put out. Although tempted to toss the rose in the trash, she decided to keep her coworkers happy and show a little intestinal fortitude.

However, she was irritated with herself that she could give in so easily to Jake over a silly flower. She placed the vase on her desk. Under the overhead lights, the crystal sparkled like a giant diamond, and the rose filled her office with its scent. She forced a smile and admitted to herself that Jake looked more handsome than she remembered. But how did he find her? What was he doing in the Army…and in Berlin, no less? And man did he look lip-smacking good in that uniform.

Too bad he was a total loser.

***

The following day, a different deliveryman came by the office, looking for Marianne. He held a colorfully wrapped package, similar in size to the one she had received the previous day. Inside, there was another long-stemmed rose, a pure white one this time but without the vase. The attached note simply read: *Until we meet again. Love, Jake.*

The next day, the next, and the next one after that, messengers came to the office, each one delivering another rose to add to her vase, each one a different color. Marianne wondered how long Jake's groveling would go on.

Her coworkers crowded into her office and lambasted her with questions again. "Why don't you go out with him? Can't you see he's crazy about you? Don't you have any feelings for him?"

"Listen, everyone." Marianne threw up her hands in frustration. "Jake and I are history. I'm not going to let him hurt me again."

Carla said, "He's trying to make up for what he did to you. Why not talk to him about it? Find out what happened."

"I don't care to know," she lied again.

"I'd give him another chance," someone put in.

Marianne ran her fingers through her hair. There wasn't anything Jake could tell her that would make any difference. Her coworkers didn't understand Jake's cruelty, and though they were only trying to be helpful and supportive, the mother-henning had to end here and now. "Carla, everybody, thanks for your concern, but I can take care of my own love life."

Nodding, Carla herded everyone out of the office and eased the door shut behind her.

Marianne hoped that would be the end of their prodding.

***

The next day, Marianne took the bus to the American military commissary to do her weekly grocery shopping. One of the many benefits for a government worker was access to the commissary. Food was a lot cheaper than buying it in German grocery stores. She flashed her Diplomatic ID card to the greeter at the front door. Since it was a weekend, the place was jammed with people.

Maneuvering her cart through an obstacle course of shoppers and crying children, she scanned the shelves. Why did the stockers keep moving the products from place to place so often? All of a sudden, her body jerked to a stop as her cart crashed into someone else's.

"Hey, lady," a man's gruff voice shouted from

behind her. "That's my cart."

"Oh, I'm terribly sorry." Marianne spun around to see whose cart she had crashed into. "I wasn't watching where I was—" Instant recognition: Jake. He must've passed up what he was looking for and left his cart in the middle of the aisle to go back...and he'd disguised his voice with the gruff growl. "You shouldn't leave your cart in everybody's way."

"Fancy you bumping into me here." Now his voice sounded sexy. His eyes glowed in adoration of her and swept from her hair to her lips to her eyes. She felt underdressed in jeans and an over-sized t-shirt. Grocery shopping clothes. After a split-second's pause, he flashed a wide grin that showed off his perfect teeth. "Literally, bumping into me. Get it?"

"Ha, ha." Marianne couldn't believe his sense of humor, as if he thought he had the right to taunt her like that. Glaring at him, she felt the skin on her neck heat to a hot blush. "I can't believe my rotten luck."

"Did you like the flowers?" he asked.

"I hated them." Marianne struggled to disengage her cart from his, but the wheels were tangled somehow.

With a flick of his wrist, Jake separated the two carts but held onto hers with a firm grip. "Dinner tonight?" His voice was steady, his smile sincere. "We can talk, that's all."

"No." Her face grew red with fury at herself for the way he affected her. She pushed him out of her way and started toward the opposite end of the grocery store. After a couple of minutes, she glanced over her shoulder to see if he was following her. No Jake in sight. She had expected him to pursue her.

She paused a moment to contemplate the strange disappointment she felt. On one hand, he seemed like an arrogant bastard, yet on the other hand, a lost little boy. She kicked herself for feeling her heart soften. *Damn it!* Was she being cruel to kick a man who was down on his emotional luck? Maybe Carla was right. Maybe it would be good to find out from Jake what happened on their wedding day. Until then, she was sure he'd never stop hounding her.

Out of curiosity, she walked her cart along the back of the store and peered up the aisles, searching for Jake. He wasn't anywhere to be found. It seemed as if he had vanished into thin air, now that she wanted to talk to him as much as he wanted to talk to her. And that irritated her more.

***

Over the next few days, Marianne didn't receive any more roses. Perhaps the florist ran out of colors. Or perhaps their commissary encounter had finally given Jake the message that she didn't want to see him. She bit her lip and frowned at the possibility of never seeing him again, never finding out why he'd left her at the altar. She'd lived this long since the disastrous wedding without knowing, but...

Disappointed and a bit angry at his ability to give up on chasing her so quickly, she pushed back feelings long held in check. She was surprised to discover that she had begun to enjoy Jake's attentions.

And now she had finally driven him away.

***

The downtown area of Berlin had always been a fabulous place to shop. Although bargains were a challenge to find, Marianne enjoyed window shopping. She would eventually find the *perfect dress* at a reasonable price in one of the many boutiques. Her once meager wardrobe had grown considerably, and as she adjusted her wide brimmed hat, she reflected on how she had grown to love, even crave, European accessories.

Having completed her grocery shopping the day before, clothes shopping was always a nice change of pace. She caught a glimpse of her reflection in one of the store windows. Her apricot dress hugged her small waist and swirled around her legs in the warm afternoon breeze. The chiffon material felt as luxurious as it looked, and she enjoyed the admiring glances from young men passing by. She felt empowered with her heady combination of beauty and success.

Berlin had been a lifesaver for her.

A motion in the reflection caused her eyes to focus on a figure behind her. She recognized the tall masculine form. Whirling around, she shouted, "Mr. Jake Adams, why are you following me?"

Jake, in his smart Army uniform, smiled as if he was pleased he had succeeded once more in affecting her. "I want you back, Marianne." He leaned in close and whispered in her ear. "But before that can happen, I need to explain everything, and I think you'll understand that what happened couldn't have been predicted and couldn't have been stopped. I think you'll forgive me and we can start over. I hope, anyway."

Feeling dizzy, Marianne fought to keep her wits about her. What made him think she'd ever understand? Ever forgive him. Ever start over. The thought made her stomach turn sour. She had to get away from him. "Leave me alone." With one hand, she pressed her hat to her head and stormed off.

"You want to know what happened, don't you?" he called after her.

"No. Don't bother me anymore."

After running a block, she turned into a store and placed her hand on her heaving breast, her heart beating as if she had just completed a marathon. It wasn't the getaway that had winded her. It was Jake.

***

After the unexpected meeting, a few days went by with no word from Jake. Trying to figure out why he commanded so much of her thoughts, Marianne relaxed alone in her office. She leaned back in her chair and gently played with a new leaf of a Ficus tree on her desk. Slowly Jake's image materialized in her mind. She began to twirl her hair between two fingers.

What is he doing today? This minute?

To sway her thoughts, her heart suggested that if she saw him just once more, perhaps even went out with him on just *one tiny date*, she'd learn why he'd left her at the altar. And then, once she learned the reason and reaffirmed that he was a jerk, she could get over him, once and for all.

The office telephone's tone startled her, causing her to jump and slam her left knee against the desk. "Ouch." She scowled as she picked up the receiver. "Yes, Carla, what is it?" Her voice came out strained with annoyance, and besides, her knee hurt.

Carla said, "My, my, aren't we in a fine mood? Maybe I should tell Jake that you are too busy to talk to him right now."

"Ummm..." *He's giving you another chance, Marianne. Don't blow it...* "No. I'll take the call."

"Line three."

Marianne grimaced as she punched the flashing yellow button that had Jake on hold. "Marianne Tucker," she said in a professional manner. "How may I help you?" As much as she wanted to deny it, her heart flipped over with the anticipation of hearing his smooth voice. It took complete self-control to keep her voice cool and business-like.

"Allow me the pleasure of your company at dinner tonight." His voice overflowed with self-confidence.

Determined to follow her new direction with him, she replied, "I've been thinking, Jake..." She twisted the phone cord around her fingers. "I would like to get this over with, once and for all. If I agree to go out with you and let you explain why you left me standing at the altar, will you agree to never bother me again?"

"Never?"

"You heard me."

"But never is forever."

"You should try standing at the altar waiting for your groom. Forever is easy."

"All right. Give me a chance to explain what happened, I'll never pester you again."

"Any funny business, if you don't live up to your end of the bargain, I'll get you arrested for stalking."

"I'll pick you up at 8:00 sharp."

"Jake, I haven't told you where I live."

"I already know."

She gasped. "Have you been spying on me?"

He chuckled and ended the call with a cheerful, "See you tonight."

Staring at the receiver still in her hand, she noticed Carla enter the office.

"Well?" Carla grinned, standing with her arms crossed. "What did he want?"

"Dinner."

"And you told him no again?"

Marianne replaced the receiver on the hook. "No. I told him yes."

"Good for you."

"I'm only going out with him for two reasons. Number one, I want to find out why he stood me up at the altar, and number two, after dinner, he's agreed to leave me alone forever. I'll be rid of him for good."

Carla tisked. "Sure you will."

She did not sound the least bit convinced.

Chapter NINE

8:00 pm. Date night.

Marianne's heart fluttered like a caged bird. She guessed this was, in a sense, a first date with Jake. It had been a long time since she went out on a formal date with anyone, but this time she was going to maintain absolute control over her emotions and not let him affect her the way he had in the past.

She looked in the bathroom mirror and carefully checked to ensure everything was in the right place: eyeliner, lipstick, bra straps hidden. Spinning around on black high heels, she enjoyed how her skirt's black material felt against her bare legs. She had selected a white blouse with soft ruffles along the neckline. Also, she'd taken extra care in her makeup application, adding an extra dash of blue eye shadow along with a heavier-than-usual flair of dark eyeliner. The complete package made her look fabulous.

"What shall I do tonight?" she mused out loud and moistened her lips. "Shall I drive him crazy with desire and leave him hanging?" She smiled at the evil devil on her left shoulder, feeling vengeful. *Let him see what he'd missed out on all this time.* But the good angel on her right shoulder admonished her for even thinking about revenge. *He's not worth the effort.* Still, she felt vindictive for the hurt and anger he'd left her with on their wedding day.

Footsteps approached her front door and paused, sending shivers up and down her spine. The doorbell rang. Her pulse pounded in her ears. She felt as if her heart would leap out her chest. "Breathe," she told herself and took several deep breaths in an attempt to calm her shivers. "Breathe—"

The doorbell rang again.

She had to force her feet to walk and not run to the door. Her high heels click-clacked across the wooden floor. She placed her fingers on the handle and hesitated.

What will tonight bring? How will I feel about him at the end of the evening, after he tells me why he hurt me like that? What could he possibly say to make it all right? Not a damn thing.

Apprehension churned inside her like a Texas tornado. She inhaled one more deep breath and slowly opened the door, just a crack.

Her breath caught in her throat.

Oh, my God. Jake looks better than ever.

Warmth rose from her core.

He wore a gray blazer over a cream-colored shirt, which accentuated his broad shoulders. His chest tapered down to a flat stomach, and his slacks were pressed into a sharp edge. Shoes polished to a gleaming shine. Perfect.

"May I come in?" His voice shattered her straying thoughts, and when she looked up to his face, he grinned as if he didn't have a problem in the world. His eyes shimmered with an inner glow of excitement. "Marianne? Are you all right?"

She felt embarrassed for gawking, and realizing that she had only opened the door enough to identify her visitor, she opened it the rest of the way. "Hello, Jake," she said flatly in an attempt to recover her *cool*. "Come in."

Jake brushed by her. His cologne tangled her senses. With his back to her now, he couldn't see her close her eyes and inhale his delicious aroma. By the time he turned around to face her, her cool composure took control. She didn't want to let him see how he affected her, how her heart raced at his nearness, how her emotions lost sight of the past, how her lips yearned for his kisses. She reined in her raging desires by reminding herself:

I'm only going to dinner to hear him out. Besides, he has already agreed to leave me alone after this.

But is that what I really want?

Although her thorough perusal lasted a split second, Jake relished her assessment of him.

The momentary flicker of desire in her eyes displayed proof of her interest. And as she moistened her lips with her tongue, it took everything he had to not take her in his arms and kiss her, make her desire him the way he desired her.

He caressed her with an admiring gaze. She looked exquisite in that black outfit, and her long golden hair made him ache to comb his fingers through its soft, glimmering mass. But for now he had to maintain control over his intense desire for her.

"Would you like a drink?" she asked a little breathlessly.

Looking into her blue eyes, Jake considered how to dispel the momentary tension, mostly his, in the room. His jaw twitched. "No thanks. Your beauty is enough to intoxicate me."

That earned him an odd look from Marianne.

I shouldn't have let Doug talk me into this. Get a grip on yourself, Jake. Don't sound like such an idiot.

Marianne didn't know how to take that caddish remark. She frowned and gathered up a light evening sweater and umbrella. Jake opened the door and led her outside. After locking the apartment, she slipped her hand into the crook of his elbow and allowed herself to be escorted to his car. There was no turning back now.

She glanced up and down the street. Several cars were lined up along the front of the apartments. "Where did you park?"

Jake motioned with his free hand toward a red Porsche. "Right here."

"When did you get this?"

He helped her into the car. "It's a promotion gift to myself."

"Promotion?" She admired the car's leather interior.

Jake always did have a taste for the finer things.

"I just made 1st Lieutenant."

"Congratulations."

Jake beamed as he settled in behind the wheel. He started the engine, gunned the gas a couple times, and tore away from the curb.

As he drove downtown along the busy Ku'damm, she noticed the city was bustling with energy, as if it were ramping up for some big event. The sun began to set. Sidewalks filled with young couples walking hand-in-hand, restaurant workers placed large menu boards just outside their front doors, and the streets became more traffic congested by the minute. "Looks like everyone is out on a date tonight, as well." She laughed.

Jake glanced at her. "It's good to hear your laughter again and feel you close to me. God knows I've missed you."

God may have known, but I didn't.

Finding an open parking spot along the busy boulevard was impossible, so Jake chose a parking garage a couple of blocks from the restaurant.

Parked and out of the car, she strolled arm-in-arm down the busy sidewalk with Jake. Night was settling in and filled the sky with a velvety sheen. A full moon rising on the horizon chased away the last golden rays of sunset. A cool breeze rustled through lush treetops, and then gently washed over couples sitting cheek-to-cheek on benches along the tree-lined boulevard. At one point, the breeze gathered enough intensity to cause Marianne's skirt to flutter about, and she had to grasp it to keep her undies from showing.

Jake laughed and gestured forward with his hand. "We'll be inside in a minute."

"What a shame. It's such a beautiful night."

He guided her through a large pair of glass doors that led into a tall building. In the lobby, she paused before a mirror to straighten her windblown appearance.

"This is the Europa Center," he explained. "It's like a big shopping mall in the States."

She looked around. Down the huge expanse, store after store sold everything from clothes, to shoes, to books, to jewelry, to tourist souvenirs. Although the stores had already closed for the day, she made a mental note to find this place again when she could spend more time window shopping.

"I hope you'll like my restaurant choice." Jake took her arm, his grasp firm yet gentle. "Watch your step." He guided her around a wet spot on the floor.

He approached Tiffany's, which was well known for its unique atmosphere. The restaurant was situated on several long tiers that overlooked lush vegetation on each level. On one of the lower tiers, a fountain composed of funnel-shaped leaves rose from the center of a shallow pool. The leaves bent and swayed as they caught water from above and spilled it onto the leaves below, filling them until they dumped the water into the pool. Each leaf bounced back up once the water was released, animating the fountain like a real plant rustling in a breeze. The constant flow and splashing of water filled the atrium with sound.

She walked beside Jake, hand-in-hand up the steps past various tiers of dense tropical plants and cozy tables. He was looking for a cleared table, as the service here was *seat yourself*. She spotted a table underneath a lush tree where a couple was preparing to leave. Jake must have seen it at the same time. "Let's nab that one."

As soon as they settled in, a waitress walked up and handed them a menu. In German, Marianne ordered a glass of Riesling but was surprised when Jake ordered orange juice.

"Your German is quite good," he said. "I know just enough to get into trouble."

As she laughed, a small voice reminded her that if she wasn't careful, she could very easily fall for him again. If only he hadn't dumped her at the worst possible time. That was unforgivable. Keeping her original purpose in mind, she fought off her swaying emotions and concentrated on the menu.

The waitress returned with their drinks and took their orders. Once she left, Jake reached across the table and took Marianne's hand. The warm touch of his firm clasp made her jump, almost spilling her wine.

"You're beautiful, even when you're nervous," Jake whispered as he gazed into her eyes, warming her, calming her. Then he added, "I want to tell you what happened that day."

Nodding, she bit her lip in angst. Her imagination had given in to all kinds of reasons why he didn't show up, and now that she was finally about to get the truth, she wasn't sure she was fully prepared to hear it. Hating him for what he'd done had been so much a part of her that she didn't think she'd know who she was once she learned the reason behind his betrayal.

Jake took a deep breath. Staring into her eyes, he started with, "Remember our rehearsal dinner? You were gorgeous in that evening dress. And when we danced together...well, that's only one of hundreds of cherished memories that kept me sane all this time."

She frowned. What did he mean by *sane*?

"That week before was magical, and I loved how we worked together to put the final touches on our wedding plans. You spent the night at your parent's house so that we wouldn't see each other before the wedding."

The memory of that night brought a smile to her lips. Her parents were so excited for them, and her mother spent all night talking with her about how to make a marriage the best it could be. But as it turned out, all her words were for nothing.

"What went wrong, Jake? We almost had it all."

Jake's face turned glum.

Marianne's mind flew from her happy memory to a sense of impending doom. She braced herself for the worst.

"Shortly before it was time for me to leave and meet you at the church, there was a knock on the door. I opened it, thinking it was you and that you might have forgotten something, but instead, two policemen barged in and arrested me."

Her mouth flopped open. *Arrested him? What in the world—?*

"I had no idea what was going on." Jake

frowned. "Before I knew it, I was handcuffed and tossed into a police car. I told them I was supposed to be getting married in an hour, there was some kind of a mistake, but they didn't care. In fact, I didn't know until Sunday what I was being charged with."

Marianne's jaw dropped. This sounded made-up. "What did you do?"

He held out his hand in a *hold on* gesture and grimaced. "And the worst thing of all was that they hauled me away so fast that I didn't have a chance to grab my wallet, or anything..." His eyes grew dark and his mouth tightened. "They say you get one phone call when you go to jail. Ha. What a joke that turned out to be. The cops ignored my demands to call you."

Marianne sat stunned in wide-eyed disbelief as Jake poured out his sorry tale of woe. "Of course you get one phone call," she said. "You expect me to believe you? There's some other reason you didn't call me."

"It's the truth." He swirled his orange juice then took a long gulp. His eyes were filled with pain. "I was stuck in that stinking cell, pacing back and forth, trying to persuade the guards to let me have my phone call. It was my wedding day, for God's sake, but they refused me each time. On Monday, the judge set my bail at $500,000."

"What did you do, kill somebody?"

"That's when they let me have a phone call. I had to get out of there, so I called my lawyer, told him to call you and my bank."

"I didn't get a call." The damn lawyer, it was all his fault.

Jake gritted his teeth. "He called the bank first, the moneygrubber, and the bank officer told him that I had withdrawn every penny from my savings and checking accounts." Jake looked at her with pleading eyes. "You've got to understand, I was in a big jam. I was flat broke, stuck in jail, and I had to sit there and rot until trial."

"What were you charged with?"

"Embezzlement."

A million thoughts flew through her mind. *What kind of man steals from his employer? Why would Jake do that? And how long had he been siphoning money from the till?* "How much did you steal?"

"I didn't steal a dime, Marianne. I was framed."

Her head began to ache. She rubbed her temples. "Why would anyone frame you?"

"I think the person who framed me was the same person who stole my money and embezzled the company's funds. Even made me lose you."

Marianne shook her head in shocked disbelief. All this time she thought he'd gotten cold feet and ran. "Who framed you?"

"I don't know."

"So why didn't you call me and tell me what happened?"

Jake cleared his throat. "My life had turned upside down. Being tossed in jail, charged with something I didn't do, my bank accounts emptied, and then I was given a crappy public defender who wasn't much help. After my arraignment, the case was set to go to trial in six months."

"You still should have called me, Jake."

"I tried. Your phone was disconnected. My letters were returned. No forwarding address."

"Oh dear." She remembered being so hurt, so mad, that she'd disconnected her phone, moved and left no forwarding address. She never wanted to speak to Jake again.

He shrugged. "What was I supposed to do?"

She sat motionless and remained silent, not knowing what to say or even how to respond. All she could do was look down at the linen tablecloth and wonder if she had overreacted. But what else could she have thought. He didn't show up for the wedding. His stuff had been cleared out of their apartment. He'd moved. He was gone. He was never coming back.

No, this wasn't my fault.

"Besides," Jake went on. "When I got out of jail, I couldn't find you. I felt ashamed that I let you down. I was so broke I couldn't afford to get married anyway. So I enlisted in the Army."

Marianne looked up at him. "Too broke to get married?"

Jake rocked back in his seat. "I figured you didn't want me to find you anyway."

"I didn't. You dumped me on our wedding day."

"There's something else I need to tell you."

The waitress returned with their dinners, but instead of appreciating the wonderful smell of the cuisine, Marianne choked on anger. "I would have understood, but you didn't give me a chance. Besides, I wasn't marrying you for your money, so even if you were broke, it wouldn't have mattered. I guess you didn't know me very well, did you?"

That realization hurt worse than hearing *The Wedding March* play for the second time as people turned in their seats and strained their necks in hopes of seeing Jake appear in the doorway. She'd stood at the back of the church with her father in total embarrassment, waiting to take her stroll down the aisle, and then finally having to admit that the wedding was a bust. Everyone went home shaking their heads in disbelief.

The memory of that day stabbed her heart with searing pain.

How could he have thought I wouldn't have understood his problems?

"You should have tried harder to find me."

"I figured you hated my guts...probably moved on, found someone new."

"You figured right."

"You found someone new?"

"No. I hated you."

Jake reached across the table and enclosed both of her hands in his. "Marianne, I have lived with the guilt of what happened that day. It has eaten me alive, but...I wondered why you didn't look for me. If you'd have filed a missing persons report with the police, you'd have found out I was in jail and could have bailed me out."

Marianne's mind reeled. She yanked her hand from his. How dare Jake turn it around on her? "I didn't file a report because there was no need for one."

Jake's eyebrows shot up in surprise. "What are you talking about?"

"When I got back to our apartment, all of your stuff was gone." Marianne's eyes burned with tears of betrayal.

"Gone?"

"Yes," Marianne hissed. "Everything. Your clothes, your books, your computer, all gone, Jake. You weren't missing. You moved out. While I was standing at the altar waiting for you, you ran like a coward."

Jake raked his hands through his hair. "Marianne, this is crazy. I was in jail. I couldn't have moved out of the apartment. When I got out six months later and went back, someone else was living there. I thought you'd thrown all my stuff in the dumpster."

"I figured you left town. What else was I supposed to think?" She folded her arms and looked off into the distance, taking all this in.

If Jake was in jail, then who took his stuff? How did the thief or thieves break in? And why only his stuff. Nothing of hers was touched.

Jake looked down as if grappling with these questions himself. He then looked at her and placed his hand on the table between them as if requesting her to hold it. "Marianne, I would *never* leave you. I can only imagine what went through your head that day. It must have been agonizing for you to think that I had abandoned you like that."

She unfolded her arms and took his hand. It felt cool, probably due to his nervous state. "Jake, I don't know what to think."

"Can you ever forgive me?"

"It's not that easy." He'd have a lot more groveling to do. She decided to change the topic. "Our dinners are getting cold."

"I'm not hungry."

"I am." She picked up her fork. After her first bite, she was pleasantly surprised at how famished she was. The beef stroganoff was delicious. But Jake's words were still eating at her.

"So you joined the Army because you were too broke to get married? That sucks, Jake."

"I know." He cleared his throat. "But I love you, Marianne. I can't live without you. Every day has been hell. And now, you being here in Berlin, us getting together like this, it's got to be divine intervention. Fate. Destiny. Celestial alignment. Don't you see? We're meant to be together."

Surprised at his emotional outpouring, she studied him carefully. His eyes told her that he truly felt sorry about the past, and she felt sorry for what they went through as well. Maybe they could make a new start, right here in Berlin. But what would that be like? Would he move in with her? She with him? Get married or just shack up?

She couldn't see that happening. There were still

way too many unanswered questions. Woman's intuition suggested there was more to the story than he'd told her. But what had he left out? He wouldn't have run off to join the Army just because he was too broke to get married.

Before this evening, she had anticipated listening to a weasel of a story, and that would be the end of it. He'd go his way. She'd go hers. But now things seemed different. She felt different. Her mind cautioned her.

Don't be in a rush. Take your time. Get to know him again.

She considered the inner warning then looked into his eyes and squeezed his hand. "I can't promise anything, Jake, but let's take it slow and see how it goes."

Jake's smile was so bright he could have been hearing angels sing, *Hallelujah.* "Thank you, Marianne. You won't regret giving me another chance."

She felt warmed to the core, but the voice of doubt pricked at the back of her mind.

If this doesn't work out, I'm going to hate myself for being an idiot.

Jake said, "Let's celebrate the occasion and order dessert."

Remembering the wonderful chocolate cake she and Heinrich had shared, she said, "Count me in." She finished her meal in record time.

The desserts and coffee arrived. She smacked her lips in anticipation of the first bite of luscious chocolate and strawberry cream cheesecake.

"I see that you've already grown a taste for German pastries," Jake said and sipped his coffee as he watched her enjoy her dessert.

It's better than sex.

He cut a small bit of his chocolate and strawberry cheesecake with his fork and offered it to her across the table.

"Don't you like it?"

"I love it, but this is for you...from me."

"Put it right there." She pointed to a vacant spot on her plate.

Jake's voice became playful. "Pretend it's our wedding cake."

A little taste of what she'd missed, what could be the harm? Grinning, she closed her eyes and felt his fork brush across her parted lips. She opened her eyes and attempted to take the offered bite, but he pulled it out of reach, and then waved it in front of her. Laughing, she reached with one hand to take the fork, but Jake evaded her grasp.

"Ah, ah, ah. Be patient. It'll come to you."

She loved the way he teased her. "Don't make me beg."

"Open up."

Closing her eyes, she opened her mouth to await the tasty morsel, which she planned to snatch off the fork before he could pull it away.

Jake touched the cheesecake to her upper lip as if testing for a trap, but she remained still.

"That's more like it."

Gentle as a surgeon, he slipped the tidbit into her mouth, but instead of chomping down on it and ruining the romantic moment, she closed her lips over the fork and moaned in pleasure, not only for the dessert's wonderful flavor, but also for Jake's romantic gesture.

He withdrew the fork, and she opened her eyes. His eyes had a soft glow to them. She ran her tongue along her lips to get every crumb. That made his eyes smolder with desire. And she was not unaffected. Warm butterfly wings fluttered in her stomach. The combination of wine, a wonderful dinner, and a marvelous dessert with a man as handsome and caring as Jake had relaxed her and rekindled her desire.

After dinner, Jake took her hand and led her outside for a stroll along the Ku'damm. Her heart felt like a dove beating its wings. Her mind began to broadcast warning messages.

Take it easy, girl, remember, nice and slow. Don't fall for him fast. You really don't know him. You could get hurt again.

She shook off her negative thoughts, slammed the door on those warning voices, and tossed the key.

"This is so beautiful." She sighed as she pointed to the glittering tree-lined boulevard.

He paused under a streetlamp and tilted her chin up. "Yes, it is." The softness in his voice meant he was referring to her beauty. As his lips closed in on hers, she turned away, and with her heart pounding, she pointed out some designer clothes in a nearby display window. "Look."

Her inner voices had found the tossed key and shouted warnings once more.

"These clothes are so fabulous but incredibly expensive." She pointed to one gown in particular. It was a creamy white Ralph Lauren taffeta formal, trimmed with lace and thousands of Swarovski rhinestones that sparkled like diamonds. She peered at the price tag and then looked at Jake who appeared to be confused. "That one dress costs as much as I make in a month."

Jake nodded. "Yeah, but it would look great on you."

She wanted to fall into his arms and tell him she was sorry for the put off, but that would mean she loved him too, and if someone hooked her up to a lie detector and asked her if she loved him, if she could ever love him again, the machine would blow a fuse. Instead, she said, "It's getting chilly," and rubbed her arms.

He removed his jacket and draped it around her shoulders. "I thought you wanted me to kiss you. I would have never—"

"It's me. It's my fault, Jake. I'm not ready yet." She fought to sort out her raging emotions and silence those warning voices. "Take me home."

He took her hand and walked her toward the car. "Do you still dance?" His low voice broke the awkward silence.

"I haven't danced with anyone since you left."

"Marianne..." He cleared his throat. "Are you

involved with someone else?"

That came out of the blue. "No...not really."

"What does that mean? Not really." Jake pulled her to a stop and faced her. "I need to know."

"What makes you think—?"

"Someone told me they saw you with another man."

Heinrich, it had to be Heinrich, but he was just a friend. "Are you spying on me again?"

"I just don't want to come between you and someone else."

She felt her face flush. He was being considerate to a fault. "Really, Jake, I'm not seeing anyone."

His face broke out in a broad smile. "In that case, how would you like to go with me to the Officer's Ball? It's two Saturdays from now."

"Jake." Her voice came out high pitched and breathless with dread. He was talking about an official date, one that would take her into his territory. His Army friends would be there. All eyes would be on her. She wasn't ready for that kind of exposure with him. A movie, maybe, a picnic, but the Officer's Ball? "I'd love to. But I don't think so."

"Why not?"

"I wouldn't know what to wear," she lied.

"All you have to do is look beautiful, as usual. We'll have a great time."

"I've never been to a military ball." She looked up at him and watched his eyes fill with desire.

He held his breath and pressed in closer.

Her knees went weak, and her breathing grew

deeper. At that moment, all she wanted was to feel Jake's lips pressing against hers.

But Jake was a quick learner. He closed his eyes and lightly kissed her on the forehead, as if he wanted to savor every moment with her and start a slow courtship, exactly what was needed to rebuild what they once had.

He took her hand and continued walking down the sidewalk. "Let me know when you change your mind."

She felt bemused by his mild affection, but welcomed the fact that the sexual pressure was relieved, though her body ached for his touch. The thought of him kissing her warmed her heart, but she was not going to rush into another romance with him until she was sure he'd told her the real reason he'd run off to the Army. Her jumbled emotions confused her: she wanted him now, she wanted him to wait, she wanted him...*right* now. The least she could do was accept his invitation to the ball.

Jake drove her back to her apartment. He didn't say much. His emotions must have been confusing him, as well. After walking her up the steps to the front door, he embraced her and pecked her on the cheek. "I'll call you tomorrow morning."

"Jake. I'll...I'll go to the Officer's Ball with you."

"You will?"

"I'll find something to wear."

"You've just made my day, Marianne."

"Goodnight, Jake."

"Sweet dreams." He skipped down the steps to

his car, did a happy jig, got in and drove off.

She felt stunned at his quick departure. It seemed he'd taken the air she breathed with him and left her standing in a void.

"What am I doing to myself?" she whispered as she watched the Porsche's taillights fade into the night.

Chapter TEN

MORNING SUNLIGHT POURED through Marianne's bedroom windows, bathing her with golden warmth. Her radio alarm came alive with a classical piece by Mozart. She sat up in bed and yawned and stretched. The memory of the previous night made her smile. Despite her earlier concerns, she had survived a dinner date with Jake. More surprisingly, she'd accepted his explanation of why he'd left her standing at the altar. However, his reason for not trying harder to find her, because he was too broke to get married, still didn't sit right with her. There was something else, some other reason than money that he'd run off and joined the Army.

The image of Jake in a striped prison uniform made her shudder. Who had put him there...and why? Who had stolen his money and removed his belongings from their apartment? And why didn't Jake try to find answers to those questions? Or had he known all along and neglected to tell her last night?

Needing to chase out uncomfortable images of Jake's situation, she jumped out of bed, determined to focus on happy thoughts. She was going to go to her first Officer's Ball.

***

As soon as she stepped inside the Passport Office, she was bombarded from every angle with questions about the previous evening's activities.

"How was it? Where did you go? What did you do? Are you going to see him again?"

Marianne pretended to be indifferent, which tortured her coworkers. She showed them a wan smile to disguise her true joy and sauntered into her office, which sent them a conflicting message to further heighten their curiosity.

The phone rang.

Back to work. She picked up. "Yes, Carla?"

"It's him."

Marianne's heart rate jumped.

"Should I tell him to quit calling? He's not supposed to bother you anymore, right?"

Carla wouldn't understand. "Patch him through."

"Marianne, you didn't—"

"Please."

"I knew it." The phone clicked over to the incoming call.

"Marianne Tucker."

"Hi." Jake's voice sounded pumped with excitement.

"You're chipper this morning?"

"Thanks again for last night. I really enjoyed your company."

She noticed Carla peeking in the doorway and shooed her back to work. "Yes, it was nice seeing you again." Marianne bit her lip and added, "and you looked handsome as ever."

"Thanks. And you were simply stunning."

She felt her cheeks blush. All this small talk, *but that's what courtship is all about.*

"Did you sleep well?"

She'd tossed and turned and punched her pillow and thought about him all night, but she told him, "Fine, yes, I did."

"You haven't changed your mind about the Officers Ball, have you?"

She imagined him on the other end of line, chewing the phone cord or his fingernails, pacing his office, maybe even sweating. The image of a nervous Jake made her smile. "If I change my mind, you'll be the first to know."

"Great. But in the meantime, I'm wondering about something else."

"Don't worry. Whatever I find to wear won't embarrass you."

"No, it's not that. It's about *this* Saturday. Would you like to go boating with me on the Wannsee?"

"What's the Wannsee?" Marianne furrowed her brows.

"It's a lake just southwest of the downtown area. Are you free?"

Although she wanted to shout yes at the top of her lungs, a sudden thought stopped her. Boating? That meant she'd have to wear a bathing suit. A bikini. Show him lots of skin. She wasn't sure she was ready to go that far with him, but then he'd be wearing his swimsuit. An image of him in a Speedo made her contemplate the view she'd be getting in return. A heat wave rushed over her, but she played it cool. "Let me check my calendar. What time are you talking about?"

"I'll pick you up at eleven o'clock in the morning."

She flipped pages on her desktop calendar loud enough for him to hear the paper rustle, and then, "Looks like I'm available."

"Great. It'll be fun."

"I'm looking forward to it."

"Gotta run now, chat with you soon."

"Bye."

The phone clicked dead. She felt as if she was floating on air and wanted to count down the minutes until she'd see Jake again.

**

Saturday morning, Jake arrived promptly at 11 am. He'd packed a lunch bag of tuna salad sandwiches, chips, and brought a couple soft drinks in a small cooler. The weather was sunny and cool. Marianne felt comfortable in her strappy sundress with matching sandals and purse. She left her bikini in the drawer. No free shots for him today. Just as well. He wore Dockers and a polo shirt. No free shots for her either.

He started the drive to the Wannsee. The throaty purr of his Porsche matched her contented mood. When he pulled the car onto the highway, he turned up the radio.

She leaned back in her seat and studied him. His lean, tanned arms contrasted against his blue Polo shirt. His bronzed hair fluttered in the breeze from his open window. Long lost feelings began to well up in her belly, causing her to blush and look at the road ahead.

Jake lowered the radio volume. "You'll love the Wannsee. It's one of several lakes in Berlin. The Glienicke Palace is nearby, and if we have time, we can stop by and check it out. There's even a Berlin-American Yacht Club that several members of my staff belong to. They tell me how much fun they have every weekend practicing for races against the French and British teams."

Before Marianne could ask about the Gliencke Palace, Jake chattered on in tour-guide mode. "The Wannsee has the longest inland sandy beach in Europe." He hung his arm out his window and grinned, his eyes sparkling with his next tidbit of information. "There's also a portion of it that's a clothes-free zone."

Marianne stared at him. *Was he joking?* There was no way she was going to *go native*.

"I'm serious. There really is a nude beach." He'd said it like he actually played with the thought of the two of them without clothes, walking hand-in-hand along the shore.

"Don't get any ideas." She tugged her dress over her knees.

Jake chuckled and returned his attention to his driving. Soon the car approached a sparkling blue-green marina filled with boats of all shapes and sizes. The air smelled fresh and clear, and Marianne enjoyed viewing the beautiful combination of green forest and tan beach on the opposite side of the marina.

Looking over rows of moored boats, she gestured toward the docks. "Which one is ours?"

"That one over there." He pointed to a large tour boat that had just lowered the ramp for passengers who'd formed a line, ready to embark.

"It's a two-hour cruise." He opened her door. As she climbed out, he stepped in close to her and shut his eyes as if he were savoring the essence of her perfume.

"We're going to miss the boat," she said to snap him back to his senses.

"Oh." He pulled a brochure out of his back pocket and handed it to her. "I can't read German. Would you please translate?"

She smiled at the opportunity to show off her German language skills. While reading the brochure out loud, she described the names of the different lakes and landmarks they would be visiting. "The Kleiner Wannsee, Stölpchensee, Kohlhasenbrück, Griebnitzsee, Glienicke Bridge, Moorlake, Pfaueninsel, then we'll take the river Havel back to Wannsee."

"You're a good translator." He retrieved the small cooler and sack lunch from behind the seat.

"I see the word *Pfaueninsel,* which means Peacock Island. Are we going to see peacocks there?"

"King Frederick William the Second had the Pfaueninsel Castle built for him and his mistress in 1793. His successor, Frederick William the Third, modified the island's buildings and added a menagerie based on the one he'd seen in Paris. He kept several exotic animals, including peacocks. They still roam the island today."

"I can't wait to see them."

Jake led her toward the tour boat. He held her close and whispered into her ear, "I'm so glad you could make it today. This is going to be a fun trip."

She stashed the brochure in her purse and paid very close attention to her footing as they walked up the gangway. Even though it seemed secure, the craft rocked as passengers boarded.

There were two main sections. The open-air upper level sported rows of bench seats that provided passengers with a panoramic view of the scenery, but the deck was windier than the inside level, where passengers viewed the vistas by looking out the windows.

Jake paused at the stairway to the boat's upper deck. "Inside or outside?"

"Definitely outside." She wanted an unobstructed view of everything around her.

"Then follow me." Jake led her up the narrow staircase and claimed two seats by the railing.

"Look over there." She pointed to the shoreline where a young woman stood knee-deep in the water. Several swans paddled around her as she tossed pieces of bread to them.

Marianne whipped out her camera and snapped a picture of the peaceful scene.

The boat's horn blasted, indicating the journey was about to begin. At the unexpected sound of the noise, she jumped in surprise, and then snuggled cozily into Jake's side. He grinned as if delighted that things were going so well.

"I'm hungry." She shot an obvious glance at the sack lunch. At least she hoped it was obvious.

Jake dusted off an adjacent bench and laid out their lunch. The tuna salad sandwiches smelled heavenly. He handed her one.

She took a bite. Her stomach rejoiced. "This tastes great."

"I slaved in the kitchen for hours," he quipped and handed her a cold soda from the cooler. "Something to wash down that sandwich."

She accepted the soda and took another big bite of her sandwich. "This tastes as good as the gourmet meal we had on our dinner date." She reached for a napkin and sat up straight to dab the corners of her mouth.

Jake laughed. "Go ahead and enjoy your meal. I've got more sandwiches if you want."

Feeling relieved that her behavior wasn't too crass, she swallowed a gulp of soda and wondered how he could have thought that being broke would have made any difference to her. What a lame excuse to join the Army.

"Chips?" He tore into a bag of Doritos.

"Thanks. Your tuna salad is fabulous."

"My specialty, being a bachelor and all."

The tour boat lumbered backward from the dock then edged its way to the right. Once situated in open water, the engines revved. Gulls fluttered in the breeze overhead, cawing and begging her to toss chips in the air for them to catch in mid-flight, which she did and laughed at their quick reflexes and athleticism.

The boat motored toward one of the many narrow rivers that separated the lakes. A German flag with three horizontal bands of black, red, and gold flapped and snapped from a tall mast on the bow.

Jake gazed at her with an amazed look in his eyes, as if mesmerized by her long hair as it flew wildly in the wind.

She struggled to keep the wayward locks out of her face as she finished the last of her sandwich. *Nothing like getting a mouthful of hair.* She downed the last of her soda. "That hit the spot."

"Glad you enjoyed it." He packed away the wrappers and empty cans while she gazed at the passing scenery.

The boat's tour guide cleared his throat on the loudspeaker and began providing information about their tour. Since he spoke in German, his words meant little to Jake, so Marianne was pleased to translate for him. Whenever the tour guide took a break, lively German music played over the speakers, which made the trip more festive.

Throughout their tour, the boat traveled through several wide canals and was lifted up and down by channel locks.

Jake asked, "Did you know Berlin has nearly 200 kilometers of waterways? It even has more bridges than Venice, more than one thousand."

"Wow. I didn't know that." She was impressed by Jake's energy and excitement and put her arm around his waist as the boat journeyed along the scenic waterways.

Noticing an elderly couple nearby, she asked in German if they would be kind enough to take their picture. After a brief nod from the wife, the husband smiled and took the offered camera.

Marianne and Jake posed with arms around each other, and Jake took that moment to tip her chin up and look into her eyes. Gulls fluttered behind them. The camera clicked, and that image was preserved, not only on film, but it was also etched in her memory forever.

The boat made several short stops at various islands, including Peacock Island, where indeed hundreds of peacocks roamed freely. Jake had brought along some dried bread in a small bag, retrieved it from the lunch sack, and handed it to Marianne.

"Here, you can feed the peacocks."

Surprised at the unexpected bag of bread and Jake's thoughtfulness, she grabbed his polo shirt collar and pulled his face down to her level. "I'd rather feed you some kisses instead."

Which she did, and the peacocks went hungry.

***

After the scenic tour, the boat returned to the dock. As Marianne and Jake prepared to leave their seats, she double-checked around her to ensure she had all her belongings, and then she took his hand. "Thanks, this was wonderful," she whispered into his ear.

"Watch your step going down."

Once off the boat, she was relieved to stretch her legs on solid ground. Two hours was a long time to sit on a boat bench, even if it was an interesting ride.

Jake drove them by the Berlin-American Yacht club where they visited the small clubhouse and looked at the racing boats. Taking her hand, he led her down a ramp to a moored skiff. "This is one of our racing sailboats, a Cal-20." He helped her over the gunwale, steadying her so she wouldn't fall overboard. "These are tiny but fast."

Once aboard, she sat on the plank seat and felt right at home. There was no one around. That niggling question came back with a vengeance. If this wasn't the right time and place to ask him, there never would be a right time and place. "Jake, I've got to ask you something."

He sat on the plank seat in front of her. "Sure, anything."

She looked into his eyes. "What's the real reason you ran off and joined the Army?"

"I told you, I was broke."

"Come on, Jake. I've always been a simple girl, low maintenance. I loved you so much I'd have slept with you in a cardboard box. I can't believe you didn't know that about me. Tell me the real reason you gave up on me...gave up on us."

His eyes grew dark and his jaw twitched. "That's not something I want to talk about right now."

"But I need to know."

He took a deep breath. "Why, when we're having such a great day, would you want to bring this up now? Can't we just continue to have a nice day and leave it at that?"

"But I have so many questions. Who framed you? Who stole your money? Who cleaned your stuff out of our apartment? Why did you run away and not go after the person who caused you all this trouble? And most of all, why didn't you come to me for help?"

"I was innocent. I got my freedom back. The money was gone, you were gone. Why can't the past be the past? I don't want to dig up old bones."

"If you don't, you're not the man I thought you were."

Jake turned his back to her and looked off in the distance.

She felt confused and disappointed at his evasive reaction, but she wasn't letting up. "You better talk to me about this," she pressed. "If you want to rekindle our relationship, then I need to know everything."

The only sound was the gentle lapping of water against the hull and the low calling of birds heading home to roost for the night. At his continued silence, she became more irritated. She wasn't about to put her heart on the line for this guy again unless he was honest with her. And she'd bet he already knew the answers to her questions. "What are you hiding?"

"It's the past, Marianne. Please leave it alone."

"I think you know who framed you."

"I don't know—"

"Don't lie to me. You're protecting whoever it was."

"I'm not."

"You expect me to believe that? You ran, Jake. That's not like you. Whatever you're hiding, it's got to be a doozy."

Thunder rumbled in the distance.

"Look. When I'm ready…if I'm ever ready to talk about any of this, you'll be the first person I come to, but I don't want to talk about it now." He stood and steadied himself with a hand on the mast. "Come on, let's start back for the car. It's going to rain."

She peered up at the gathering dark clouds. "You're going to lose me again, Jake."

"Don't say that." He helped her out of the boat. "There's nothing else you need to know. Look forward, not backward. We have our whole lives in front of us and nothing but heartbreak behind us."

She wasn't worried about the heartbreak behind them. She was worried about the heartbreak to come.

"We better run." He glanced skyward. "Or we're not going to make it." Then he led the way, sprinting up the boat ramp and across the parking lot.

A brilliant flash of lightning split the sky, followed by the crack of thunder. The storm was right on top of them. Rain let loose in sheets. Berlin's weather at its finest, and as if she wasn't having enough trouble keeping up with Jake's long-legged strides, he picked up speed. "Hurry!"

The rain was cold and struck her with stinging fury. Her wet dress drooped from her shoulders and stuck to her thighs. Another close call with a lightning bolt spurred her to run full out to the safety of the car. Jake held open her door and she jumped in, instantly soaking the leather seat.

"Jeeze, that lightning was close," Jake shouted over the rain pounding on the car body. He shut her door and ran around to the driver's side and fell in, dragging his long legs in after him.

She shivered, and teeth chattering, wished she'd brought a coat, a blanket, anything to wrap herself in, anything but Jake's arms.

So much for a fun day at the lake.

Jake started driving. "How about if we stop at the Wannsee-Hof Hotel and get some hot coffee? They have a nice little café famous for—"

"Just take me home."

He glanced at her. "Aren't you hungry?"

"No." She hugged herself against the cold that was biting at her flesh like a school of piranhas. If he wasn't going to tell her everything, then she didn't want to go anywhere with him.

Men are nothing but trouble.

"Have it your way." He rolled his eyes. "So I'll just take you home."

"That's what I said." She crossed her arms, growing more irritated and pouty by the second. The least he could do was turn on the heater.

She rode in silence back to her apartment. The storm had intensified into a gully washer. Even if she had chosen to speak to him, the roar from the rain on the roof would have made her voice impossible to hear.

He parked the car and started to get out, but she threw open her door, jumped out, and slammed it behind her.

Jake didn't get out of the car. He probably didn't know if he should stay seated, ask to come in, offer her a kiss, or just drive away.

Without a backward glance, she made a beeline to her front door, the rain pounding her all the way, but before digging in her purse for the key, she shivered at how rotten this day had turned out. The least she could do was thank him. She jogged back through the rain to his window and tapped on the glass.

He took his time rolling it down. "I'll have a deluxe burger, fries, and a Coke, please."

She stood there completely drenched, fighting the urge to burst out laughing. How could she stay mad at him very long? "Thanks for lunch and the cruise."

"Listen, Marianne—"

She turned and raced for her front door. Jake had gotten off easy this time.

Chapter ELEVEN

TWO DAYS PASSED and neither one had called the other. By Tuesday morning, Jake decided that enough was enough and planned a surprise visit to Marianne's office. He checked his watch. *11:30.* Still time to catch her for a quick lunch. He strolled into the Passport Office lobby with a bouquet of fresh gladiolas. It wasn't much of a peace offering, considering the fact that she'd pressed him for answers he'd refused to reveal. Telling her about Sylvia was not on his list of favorite things to do.

He found Carla eating lunch at her desk. "I'm here to see Marianne."

Carla almost choked on her sandwich as she peered up at Jake. "Nice flowers."

"Yeah, I was hoping to take her to lunch."

"Was she expecting you?"

"It's a surprise."

"Uh, she already left for lunch."

A coworker at the next desk wrinkled her nose and called out, "You're too late. She went to lunch with Heinrich."

Carla whipped her head around and shot the woman a disapproving glare, and then returned her gaze to Jake, shrugging. "Shall I put those flowers in her office?"

Jake's jaw twitched with a touch of jealousy. Heinrich must have been the guy Doug had seen her with. If Jake wasn't careful, he'd lose her for sure, if he hadn't already. "No thanks, I'll do it." He stepped into Marianne's office and set the flowers in the vase with the already wilting roses then turned around and walked out. "Carla, please tell her I'll catch up with her later."

"I'm sorry, Jake, but you should have called ahead."

"Yeah." He pushed out through the lobby's glass doors. "Where is all this going?" he muttered. If he told her about Sylvia, he would lose her. If he didn't tell her about Sylvia, he would lose her. Talk about being stuck between a rock and a hard place. Heinrich could become the big winner by default.

***

The next day, Jake decided to make another attempt to reach Marianne. He dialed her office, and after five rings, he was just about to hang up when Carla answered. "Passports. How may I direct your call?"

"It's me."

"Oh, hello, Jake."

"Is she in?"

"One moment please."

The line clicked.

"Marianne Tucker."

"Good morning, sunshine." Jake forced his voice to sound chipper.

"Thanks for the flowers yesterday." Her response sounded cool. "Sorry I missed you."

"I was hoping we could go to lunch today."

"So you've decided to answer my questions?"

"Not exactly. Are you available today?"

"Not exactly."

"Come on, Marianne. I'm sorry about the way things turned out last Saturday. But you've got to admit, you've still got feelings for me. What good will it do to dredge up the past?"

"I want the truth, Jake."

"It's painful to talk about." He shifted the phone to his other ear. "Can you hang in there a bit longer?"

"How hard is it to man-up and tell me?"

"It's not easy to explain. Please ease up a little."

"You think I'm being too pushy about this?"

"I understand you're concerned—"

"Concerned? How do you think I feel knowing you thought I was a gold-digger?"

"No, I didn't think that."

"I didn't love you for your money, Jake."

"I know that..." He should have seen the hole in that excuse he'd made up about being too broke to get married, so he'd joined the Army. It had backfired on him big time. "You're not a gold-digger. When the time's right, I'll explain."

"All right," she said with a tone of finality. "I'll wait a little longer, but don't make me wait too long. I'm not getting any younger."

And there was always Heinrich, the competition. "I'll see you Saturday night? The Officer's Ball? We're still on for that, right?"

"Seven o'clock. Don't be late."

"I'm never late."

She hung up.

Holding the phone, he gritted his teeth and thought how he'd dodged a bullet this time. Next time, he might not be so lucky. He'd better make the Officer's Ball a very special night for her, and he knew exactly where to start.

***

Thursday was Marianne's favorite day of the week. The mad rush of the earlier part of the week had died down, and now the focus was on tying up loose ends in preparation for the weekend. Her mountain of paperwork was down to a few sheets in her inbox when Carla poked her head around the corner. "Hey. You have a package." Her eyes grew wide. "A *big* package."

"Jake and his damn flowers again, what do you bet?"

"Did you get the part where I said *big* package?"

"What? A Volvo?"

Carla huffed. "Okay, not that big."

Marianne hopped out of her chair and followed Carla out to the main lobby. Coworkers had gathered around. "A mink coat," one said.

"Leather," another chimed in. "It's all the rage."

Marianne decided to play along. "Hmm, I wonder what it is."

"A wedding dress," another guessed. "From

Heinrich."

"From Jake," someone else put in. "Are you guys getting married?"

"When is the wedding?"

Marianne winced. Next they'd be guessing it was a box full of baby clothes and wondering how long she'd been pregnant.

"Now, now, girls." Carla held out a pair of scissors. "Give her some room to open it."

Looking over the package, Marianne saw a fancy, swirling logo on the wrapper, one she'd seen before, on a boutique window downtown, though she couldn't recall which one. And it was definitely a big box, long and wide. She took the offered scissors from Carla and carefully sliced through the tape on the box.

Coworkers pressed in closer, their eyes curious and eager with anticipation. Carla attempted to shoo everyone off, but Marianne said, "It's okay. Let them see what this is."

The tape was off, and as she lifted the lid, she gasped with surprise. "He didn't!"

"What, what?"

Her coworkers swooned as Marianne carefully lifted out a beautiful designer gown wrapped in protective plastic. It was the same one she had admired in the store window that night of her dinner date with Jake.

Carla whistled. "That had to set him back a wad."

The note pinned to the cover read: *Now you have*

something to wear.

"How thoughtful of him." Marianne's heart beat in wild anticipation of wearing it Saturday night and seeing Jake's reaction.

***

The evening of the Officers Ball arrived, and Marianne checked her dress in the mirror to make sure everything was perfect. Her designer gown of taffeta, sequins, and lace looked stunning on her curvy frame.

She had pampered herself earlier in the day and went to a hair salon to have her long hair swept up into a French coif, which was held in place with two glistening Mother of Pearl hair sticks. Leaning in close to the mirror, she double-checked that her makeup had been applied to perfection. Yep, she looked great, and she felt like Audrey Hepburn in the movie *Breakfast at Tiffany's.*

The doorbell rang.

Marianne jumped, almost bumping into the mirror face first. *Sheesh.* As she rushed to the front room, she felt nervous and excited at the same time.

What will Jake be wearing? How will the evening go?

She felt dizzy but steadied herself, gathered her composure, and opened the door.

One look at him and she had to catch her breath. Still, her composure dropped like a stone, tangled her tongue, weakened her knees, and let loose all those butterflies to tickle her insides. All she could say was, "Wow," as her gaze traversed Jake's body from head to toe. He looked handsome and proud in his crisp Army dress uniform. His broad shoulders sparkled with polished silver bars, and his left chest displayed two rows of colorful service ribbons. He tipped his hat while his wandering eyes assessed her, as well.

Transfixed before him, her body responded in ways they hadn't taught her in sex education at school.

"You look absolutely lovely." His voice grew husky with desire. "Are you ready to go?"

Only then did she remember to breathe. "Oh gosh…sorry. I don't know what got into me."

"That dress is absolutely perfect on you."

Her face flushed hot in response to his heated gaze. "Then I guess you got your money's worth."

"You'll be the belle of the ball."

This was definitely going to be an interesting evening. She grabbed a beaded purse and lacey hat off the entry hall table, locked the apartment, and took Jake's elbow as he led her to the car.

Before he opened the car door, she asked him, "Where are we going?"

"The Berlin Convention Center. It's not far from here."

Within a few minutes, he pulled up in front of a sprawling complex with international flags waving in the breeze, got out and tossed the car keys to a waiting valet. "Not a scratch, you hear?"

"Yes, sir."

Jake retrieved Marianne from the car. She hooked her arm under his elbow and let him lead the way into the building where a receiving line was already in progress. Her heart drummed a frantic tune. As they approached the line, all eyes were on them. She noticed that most of the officers were chatting with their wives or girlfriends. No one appeared single. She wondered if, in those cases, the usually single men had hired an escort service.

Walking alongside Jake, she felt like a queen in her exquisite gown, but the stares were beginning to get on her nerves. Feeling self-conscious, she clutched her purse like a Linus blanket. "Do you know all these people? They seem to know you by the way they are staring."

He smiled but shook his head. "I know a few of them, but they're staring because you're so beautiful. Don't be nervous. You'll be fine." As he escorted her to the ballroom door, he pointed to a serviceman standing at attention in the doorway. "That's the commander of this event. His job is to announce the name of each guest."

Jake presented him with an invitation card.

The commander examined the card and called out, "Mr. and Mrs. Jake Adams."

Marianne clenched her jaw until they got inside the ballroom then she let him have it. "What was that?" she screeched under her breath.

"I thought you'd like to hear how it sounded. Has a ring to it, don't you think?"

"I'm not your wife."

"It sure sounded good to me."

"You're impossible."

Jake found their table and assigned places, and like a true gentleman, he pulled out her chair for her. She took her seat and set her purse beside a gleaming china plate.

Sitting next to her, Jake looked around the room. His face lit up when he recognized one of his officer friends. "Hey, Doug." Jake stood and shook hands with a massive soldier who had marched up with his date. "You're fashionably late, as usual." Then he glanced at Doug's date and raised one eyebrow. "Good evening, Sally."

"Jake." She tipped her head. "I didn't know you were married."

"We're not married," Marianne blurted out.

Jake told her, "This is my good friend Lieutenant Doug Hanson and his *companion* Sally." Then to Doug and Sally he said, "Marianne and I were almost married." He placed his hand on her shoulder as if claiming her for his own or driving a point home to Sally.

"Nice to meet you." Marianne smiled at Doug.

His face beamed. "It's great to finally meet you. Jake's been talking non-stop about you for a long time."

"Gag me with a spoon," Sally said, pointing a finger at her open mouth.

Marianne assessed the younger woman. She had a pretty face and slender body, but she was wearing a 50's era high school prom dress with the bodice buttons undone enough to reveal a valley of cleavage, and her makeup was way overdone. It was easy to see she wasn't Jake's type. Then Marianne returned her gaze to Doug and gave him a genuine I'm-happy-you-are-friends-with-Jake smile.

Jake pointed to name cards on the plates to his right. "Here are your seats."

Marianne noticed Sally leering at Jake. What was up with those two? His face appeared neutral to her. He didn't react to her attention, which seemed to infuriate her. Why else would she scrunch up her eyes and wrinkle her nose at him?

The atmosphere quickly shifted to a serious tone, and the chatter of the crowd quickly died down to a murmur, raising the overall anticipation in the room. "What's going on?" Marianne asked, looking around.

"The posting of the colors," Jake whispered.

At that moment, everyone stood as if by some magical command. Jake shot up from his seat, stood at attention, and faced the Color Guard team entering the banquet room. Marianne followed his lead. Four uniformed men paraded across the room, carrying the United States flag. Everyone placed their hands over their hearts. Marianne did the same.

The flags were posted at the front of the room. The Color Guard saluted the flag, executed a crisp about-face, and marched out. Her heart swelled with patriotic pride and appreciation for witnessing this special ceremony.

As soon as the flag was posted, Jake whispered to her, "Next come the toasts. And at the end, a silent toast is performed to honor our prisoners of war and missing in action." He indicated a corner of the room where a small table had been covered in white linen. On the table lay shiny black plates, silverware, and crystal glasses ready to be used. At each place setting stood a picture frame that contained a black and white image of a soldier in uniform. Jake nodded toward the table and whispered, "It's symbolically reserved for POWs in anticipation of their return."

Marianne understood the heart-wrenching significance.

Everyone settled into their seats. Several servicemen made special toasts honoring various military personnel, leaders, and special guests. After the last toast was given, dinner was served.

Finally.

She was famished. Although not elaborate, the dinner was composed of a mixed green salad, followed by a tender braised chicken breast, whipped mashed potatoes smothered with a dark German Hunter Sauce, and a tasty selection of locally-grown vegetables.

Throughout dinner, a guest speaker, a former commander, entertained them with stories of how Berlin had changed over the years, and talked about the influence of the military in the city's political evolution.

After the speeches, dinner, and dessert were completed, the full orchestra atop an elegant stage began to play a dance piece, resulting in a gentle sea of colors swirling around the dance floor. Dresses fluttered with endless yards of chiffon that sparkled with glistening sequins. Dyed ostrich feathers adorned some hemlines, while tufts of the same hue accented delicate lace sleeves. Marianne's senses were dazzled.

A waltz started to play.

"Shall we?" Jake stood and extended his hand to her.

She took off her hat and placed it on the table. "Let's do it."

He rushed her onto the floor and held her in closed dance position. As he began the dance, she felt confident and extremely pleased that she looked equally elegant in her own lavish gown. Its light color accented with tiny Swarovski rhinestones shimmered under the bright chandeliers and reflected the light like a million starbursts.

Adoring smiles and low whispers filtered through the room as Jake whirled her around the floor. She felt gorgeous, the belle of the ball, just like he had said. Every time he swept her around and around, her dress swirled, causing onlookers to sigh with envy at the handsome couple, or so she hoped. And her heart could have stopped beating as he dipped her and smiled, and then he whisked her through the next series of flowing movements that made her feel like she was floating in heaven.

Too soon the waltz ended, and she felt winded and light-headed. But instead of escorting her back to their table, he stood behind her and held her in his arms, a stance that would keep her on the dance floor to await the next tune.

"Jake," she breathed. "You haven't lost your

dancing feet."

"Nor have you."

The band began a West Coast Swing. He shifted her into the start position. She caught her breath and followed his leads. Though she hadn't danced since Jake had disappeared, all the dance moves came back to her, especially the sexy ones, the knee bends, the eye-to-eye stops. *Mustang Sally* was a great flirting song. While strutting through a pass-by, she caught a glimpse of their table and noticed the real Sally seething, her eyes throwing daggers at her and Jake.

"What's her problem?" she asked him, nodding toward Sally.

"She's miffed because she had her sights on me, and I shot her down."

She wants to stare? I'll give her something to stare at. This will be fun.

Marianne kicked things up a notch and gave Jake her sexiest dance moves: lots of hip sway, touching, and fluttering eyelashes. She'd make *Dirty Dancing* look like a Disney flick.

Jake looked pleasantly surprised at her sexual gestures on the dance floor. He matched each of her moves with some sexy nuances of his own and led her into a double-underarm turn. She followed his lead with no problem and grinned at him, indicating the challenge was on. Who could out-sex the other before the song ended?

He led her into a tuck and triple underarm turn, freezing the movement on the music break, arms around her from behind. Marianne followed him to perfection, and as the music paused, she struck an alluring pose of her own while smiling sweetly at Jake.

This kind of dancing was the best foreplay ever.

When the song ended, folks at several tables applauded their performance. Marianne felt her cheeks blush, and Jake grinned like a man thrilled to have such a competent dance partner.

Sally must not have been able to take it anymore. As soon as the next song began, she pushed back her chair, almost tipping it over, and dragged a protesting Doug to the dance floor. "I'm not as good a dancer as Jake."

"Shut up and make sexy moves," she growled at him. "It can't be that hard."

Following Jake's performance would be difficult at best, kind of like bringing a Brahma bull to a ballet, especially since the next dance was a Fox Trot, a dance Doug didn't seem to know because he started on the wrong foot. As the orchestra's vocalist sang Frank Sinatra's version of *Come Fly with Me*, Sally shot a withering look at Marianne, smiled smugly, and then tried to lead Doug around the floor. While the two fought and stumbled through the number, Marianne clasped Jake's hand under the table and made her best attempt to suppress her laughter.

It didn't take Sally long to realize her error in trying to out-dance Marianne and Jake and demonstrated her frustration at Doug by stomping on his foot. Then she charged off the dance floor, leaving him on his own. Storming toward the table, she snarled at Marianne then grabbed her purse and huffed off toward the ladies room.

Doug ambled up to Jake. "What's the matter with her?"

He stood and patted him on the back. "You have your hands full with that one, buddy." He laughed.

"Yep." Doug shrugged and laughed too. "She's a pistol." He walked off toward the cash bar.

The rest of the evening was a blur for Marianne: dancing, drinking, dessert, more dancing, more drinking, and too soon it was midnight and time to leave. She retrieved her hat from the table and plopped it on her head. There was no saving her hairdo after all that dancing.

He handed her the beaded purse, and in her tipsy state, she fumbled it and dropped it. The flimsy clasp let go, and nearly everything inside went flying out. Lipstick, coins, compact, nail polish, all scattered about. She bent down, scrambling to roundup everything while her cheeks burned with embarrassment. "I'm so clumsy."

Jake helped her. "It's not your fault. I let go of it too soon."

What a perfect gentleman he was, to take the blame for something that was obviously not his fault. "Then be more careful next time," she said, but she couldn't restrain a laugh. Then he started laughing along with several nearby couples.

Once everything was back in her purse, he led her outside.

"Happy?" He smiled and placed his arm around

her shoulder, snuggling her close against him.

"I've never been happier." She snuggled even closer, feeling a warm sense of inner peace. There was no doubt about it. In spite of everything, she was falling in love with him all over again.

Pointing upward to a Mercedes emblem, aglow on top of the towering Europa Center building, Jake asked, "See that big sign up there?"

"Way up there? Yes, I see it. Why?"

"That's where I'm going to take you next. You'll love the view of the city from up there."

"Way up there? We're going way up there?" She wasn't so sure about this. It was late, and she wasn't sober enough to go anywhere that high up.

Pressing her close to his side, Jake said, "You're not afraid, are you?"

"Of course not." Then laughing at herself, she added, "How do we get up there?"

With a gentle nudge, Jake whispered. "Fly."

Soon she and Jake were zipping up twenty floors in a small elevator. She marveled at the speed they were traveling, ascending faster than one floor per second. Once the elevator reached the top, she breathed a sobering sigh of relief. The doors opened, and she stepped out.

On the windy terrace of the rooftop, she was rewarded with a breathtaking view. "It's beautiful." She hugged him. "We can see everything from up here."

"What did I tell you?"

She slipped away from him to look in another

direction. But just to be on the safe side, she stayed well away from the ledge and clung tight to her purse. Due to the late hour, they had the rooftop to themselves, or so it seemed.

The busy streets below glittered with multi-colored lights. Golden spotlights that shined on the 750-year-old Kaiser Wilhelm Memorial Church below made the spires appear mystical. From this high vantage point, she could see the square patterns, courtyards, and walls of the buildings below, all framed in streetlight. He pointed out the Berlin Zoo, and in the distance, she could see over to East Berlin's much darker landscape.

"What's that tower over there...shaped like a disco ball on a stick?"

"The Fernsehturm. It's a television tower built in the late sixties and still a famous landmark on Berlin's skyline."

"It's pretty cool."

He took her hand, and as she explored the views from different sides of the rooftop, a strong gust of wind blew her hat off. In an attempt to grasp it, she tripped over her own feet and almost fell down a narrow flight of stairs. But Jake held her hand tight, saving her from a dangerous, perhaps fatal fall.

"That was too close."

"I'm a little tipsy, sorry." Her nerves were frayed, but she was glad she hadn't dropped her purse.

Jake's eyes filled with fear as he held her close to him. "If you had slipped out of my hand, I would have lost you."

She shuddered at the frightened tone in his voice. "I'm all right now. You can let go. Besides, I have to fix my hair."

"Sure, of course." He stepped back.

Her hair sticks had loosened, and her upswept coif had unfurled. She pulled the sticks out and placed them in her purse, then started to gather her hair into a pony tail.

Jake clasped her hand in his. "Wait a second. I like the look, all mussed up, like you just got out of bed." Jake's voice grew husky, and he drew her closer to him. "Do you realize how beautiful you look with your hair wild and let loose like that?"

"Why no, I—"

He swooped down on her lips and kissed her. At first, it was a tender kiss, but it soon built with raw passion, and he kissed her as if he had never kissed her before or would never kiss her again. She accepted it all with an eager heart.

He tore his lips away and whispered in her ear, "Marianne, I want to make love to you."

She melted in his arms.

He delicately sprinkled her face with gentle kisses, creating a sweet torture for her, and then trailed his hot lips down her neck toward her breasts. Her senses reeled. Every cell in her body came alive and cried out his name. *Jake, oh yes...*

This was exactly what she needed, exactly what she wanted. White hot flames of passion licked the insides of her thighs and made her knees weak. Her breathing quickened, her mind grew increasingly light-headed, and her knees finally buckled. As she felt herself slide downward, Jake caught her at the waist and drew her even closer to him as her passion for him increased. She threw all sense of caution to the wind.

"Jake…"

She whispered his name over and over again. This felt too good to be true.

He returned his attention to the hollow of her throat and began to make lazy circles with his tongue around to the side of her neck.

She was on fire. Her breasts ached for his touch. Even more so for his lips to play with her nipples. She wanted him here and now, regardless if they were alone or in the midst of a thousand tourists. Her heart beat like a drum brigade. But she knew deep inside that she would not allow herself to have him this way…right here and now. If they were destined to be together, they would wait a bit longer, for the right time. The right place. Oh what the hell, just do it right here.

A strange clicking sound invaded her consciousness, ripping her from her lustful thoughts. The clicking seemed to have come from behind her. She pushed back from Jake's chest. "What was that clicking?"

He stopped kissing her long enough to say, "Must be the gears of the sign rotating above us." Then he returned to kissing her neck, but she no longer felt comfortable being this intimate in a public place, even if there seemed to be no one around.

More clicking.

In an attempt to allow her mixed emotions a little time to sort themselves out, she decided to create a distraction by dropping her purse. Just like before, the clasp didn't hold, and her things tumbled out.

Jake immediately let her go. "Oh no. Did I do that?"

"Help me." She stooped to pick up her stuff.

He joined her and drew in a ragged breath. "Marianne, I'm sorry...it's just...I lost control."

"Yeah, me too," she breathed.

"What are we going to do? We're meant to be together, but..."

"But this isn't how it's meant to be, up here, on a windy rooftop like two teenagers on prom night. And we have issues that need to be resolved before we can move forward." She closed her purse. "*Meant to be* isn't good enough, Jake."

He swallowed hard. "When you are ready, let me know. I want you to be mine forever. And this time, I will never let anything keep us apart."

Warmed by those heartfelt words, she leaned in and kissed him.

That odd clicking sound came again...from behind her, not from above.

"This isn't all about you. It's not all about me, either. It's about us. We need time to work everything out, not rush into a happily ever after until we are both ready."

"It's late. Let me drive you home."

With a curious mixture of disappointment and relief, she marveled at how good it felt to be in his arms again but wondered if she would feel the same way about him tomorrow if she had given in to their desires tonight. She didn't want to get hurt again.

As he turned her toward the elevator, she heard the clicking again and looked behind her. Movement in the shadows caught her eye, a dark figure...

"Look. Over there. That man is taking pictures of us."

Jake spun and faced a man standing a short distance away, jamming a camera into a leather bag.

"Hey, you."

The man looked at Jake, muttered a profanity, and then dashed for the stairwell.

"Stop!" Jake sprinted after him and almost managed to grab his bag strap before Jake's foot caught on the man's heel, throwing Jake off balance. He tumbled over.

Marianne thought to take up the chase but ran to check on Jake first. "Are you okay?"

The man's fading footsteps raced down the stairwell.

Jake sat up and massaged his knee where his uniform pants were torn. "Maybe I shouldn't have had that last beer. I'd have caught him."

She stared in the direction the man went. "Why would someone take pictures of us?"

"I have no idea."

But the fear in Jake's eyes told her that he may have had some idea, after all.

Chapter TWELVE

A FULL MOON SMILED down on Berlin as millions of stars twinkled above like brilliant diamonds scattered across the sky. A late night breeze fluttered through the old city streets, encouraging sleep.

It was 2:00 am, and everyone in the neighborhood was asleep except for the occupants of an upstairs room in an old boarding house. White drapes fluttered from an open window, and a faint conversation could be heard as two silhouettes stood out against the yellowish living room backlight.

One of them, a tall voluptuous woman clad in a long robe, studied some papers in her hand. The other figure facing her looked squat-bodied with a wild mass of hair sprouting from the top of his head, making him look more like a carrot than a man.

As the woman leafed through page after page, the man poked his head out through the curtains as if he were looking for a way to escape.

"Get away from the window, Damien!"

The man spun around, his right eye twitching as he waited for her assessment of his report. He had only been there a short time, and he already ached to flee. In the presence of this beautiful and powerful woman, he felt trapped like a small animal in a cage.

She made him nervous, and he didn't trust her as far as he could spit.

Hoping the information he offered would please her, he glanced down at his left hand and grimaced at the painful memory of the last time she became irritated with him and slammed the car door on his hand. She was an elegant woman, but her foul temper made her dangerous and ugly.

As the woman flipped through the report, her eyes glittered with self-satisfaction. "Very interesting," she purred while strolling back and forth across the plush carpet of this two room suite. She then placed the papers on a shelf next to a large wall mirror. "This trip to Berlin was well worth it."

Since Damien Prue's visit was unexpected, she had little time to fix her appearance. Fortunately her lover, who was waiting for her in the bedroom, didn't mind the interruption. He needed a break anyway.

She pulled her black hair up and tied it in back as she studied her informant's reflection in the mirror. His bug eyes were focused on her every move.

God, this man is ugly.

If she hadn't been so desperate for this information, she could have spent some time selecting a more handsome investigator:

And who knows, maybe I could have worked out a mutually beneficial form of payment…

A shiver of sexual excitement flittered throughout her body, and then she forced her musings back to reality. She picked up the report and strutted across the room where she slapped the papers down on the coffee table. "Why did it take you so long to find him?"

"The Army is not easy to infiltrate, madam."

Her mouth curved into a wicked smile. "I'm glad you succeeded."

"I'm happy madam is pleased."

Reaching for a pack of cigarettes on the table, she pulled one out, clamped it between her long fingers, and glared at him expectantly.

Damien patted his stubby hands on the front of his jacket and located a lighter. His forehead furrowed as he fumbled it with shaking fingers in a clumsy attempt to light her cigarette. The woman rolled her eyes, grabbed the lighter from his hand, and lit the cigarette herself. "Fool." She threw the lighter at him and inhaled a long drag.

He caught the lighter with one hand, his gun hand, his quick hand, and hoped she hadn't noticed his fast reflexes. "May we settle up now, Madam Sylvia?"

She blew smoke in his face. "I paid you a lot of money to do this simple task."

Damien blurted out in a squeaky croak, "I hope my fee is well worth your while." He winced as he flexed his hand and added, "There is no extra charge. I really thought the last guy was him…really."

Sylvia scowled then tossed her head and laughed. "Just be happy you found him before I ran out of patience." She crushed her just-lit cigarette in an ashtray, this time giving the man a blazing look as she picked up the report and waved it in his face. "So is this *all* you have on him?"

"Yes, that is it…all of it." He pushed out his chest and forced a more confident and controlled demeanor. "Madam Sylvia, I would like the rest of my money now."

Sylvia sneered. "I paid you enough money."

"Only the down payment, as we agreed."

"You owe me the balance for losing my passport."

"That was not my fault."

"You're right. It's my fault for letting you use it to sneak your whore girlfriend into the city. Took me half a day at the passport office to order a new one. Consider the balance my inconvenience pay."

"I consider that unfair."

"Very well." She stormed past him, whirled around, and threw open the front door. "Consider yourself fired."

"You will regret this. I hope he is worth it."

"He dumped me for another woman," she shrieked. "For that he will suffer the rest of his life."

"Revenge is a dish best served cold, madam."

"Get out, you worm."

Damien rushed out to the safety of the hallway.

Sylvia slammed the door and cackled with glee at her cunning dismissal of the investigator. She had no more use for him.

Returning to the bedroom, she glanced inside and discovered to her disappointment that her once energetic lover had fallen asleep.

Eh, he wasn't that impressive anyway.

Shrugging, she closed the bedroom door and padded to the mini-bar where she selected a sparkling crystal goblet into which she poured her favorite wine, a nice merlot. Carrying the report with her to the sofa, she placed the goblet on the coffee table, sat down, and curled her feet underneath her.

Hello, Jake. At last we will meet again.

She smiled. Lifting the glass of wine to her lips, she closed her eyes and took a long sip. The warm liquid felt sweet as it trickled down her throat. After a few more sips, she read through the report. "An officer in the Army, huh?" Her heart skipped a beat as her mind conjured up Jake's body in uniform. She fantasized raking her long nails through the sexy hair on his chest then pulling him on top of her, entwining her legs around his waist and pressing herself against him with fierce abandonment. They'd had some great sex together before that bitch Marianne entered the picture.

She frowned. Speaking of pictures, she studied the photos included with the report. A few showed Jake with a woman, all taken with her back to the camera.

Damn Damien. Why didn't he get a decent angle on that woman's face?

She focused on Jake who looked absolutely delicious. Yes, it would be nice to see him again. With that thought in mind, she strolled back into the bedroom and jumped on top of her sleeping lover. "Wake up, you whore. Momma's back."

***

Armed with the most recent information, Sylvia decided that today was the day to visit Mr. Jake Adams. After procuring a pass onto the Army base from one of her Congressman flunkies, she had friends in high places, she found the building where, according to the report, Jake worked. She would give him an ultimatum: dump that bitch Marianne and marry her or face her wrath again.

As she walked the gray hallways, the steely click-clack sound of her black spiked high-heels echoed off the walls. Consulting the report, she approached an office that was supposed to be Jake's. She was about to find out if her money was well spent on Damien.

Several soldiers gawked at her as she paraded her curvaceous body past them. Her black taffeta skirt flared open at the side, allowing everyone a glimpse of her long, shapely leg. And more alluring than that, her tiny waistline enhanced her full breasts, which bounced lightly underneath her olive blouse. All this, along with her raven hair flaring behind her and a black wide-brimmed hat from Paris, made her feel like a mystical goddess from the Netherworld.

As she entered the office, a quick scan of the room produced a girl, a secretary or receptionist, sitting at a desk, a row of chairs along the wall, a magazine rack, and a clutch of uniformed men gathered at a water cooler, none of whom were Jake.

How inconvenient.

The girl's eyes surveyed every inch of Sylvia, and from the scowl on her young face, she didn't seem impressed.

Stephanie Smith

However, the men were drooling over her. That was most important.

Placing her handbag on the reception desk, she examined the secretary while reaching into the bag for a cigarette. The girl seemed much too plain for Jake's tastes, short-cropped hair, enlisted person's uniform, one stripe on each sleeve. *Probably only good for getting him coffee.*

"May I help you?"

Sylvia flashed her a patronizing smile. "I'll bet you can." She withdrew a cigarette from her bag. "I'm here to see Jake."

"You can't smoke in here."

"I can do whatever I want. Now where's Jake?"

"Lieutenant Adams is not in at the moment." She said it with a growl, as if she was appalled to even have to talk to her.

Sylvia retrieved a lighter from her bag, flicked it into flame, and was about to light the cigarette when the wimpy secretary suddenly grew some balls.

"If you light that damn thing, I'll call the MPs. You'll be smoking it in a jail cell."

She held the flame an inch from the cigarette tip and glared at the snot-nosed girl.

How dare she tell me what I can't do?

"Just who do you think you are?" the girl demanded. "Strutting in here like some oversexed floozy? Jake would have you thrown out on your ass."

The servicemen at the water cooler started heading her direction. She snapped the lighter closed, killing the flame, and dropped it back into the bag, along with the unlit cigarette. "Have it your way."

The men backed off.

"This time." She expected to see Jake's coworkers a great deal in the future. No sense ruffling feathers now.

Patience, Sylvia…be patient.

"So where is he?"

Jake's secretary took a quick breath. "He's meeting with the Major."

"Well then…" Sylvia sauntered to a chair by the magazine rack. "I'll just wait for him right here."

"You'll have a long wait. He'll be gone all day."

She stopped mid-motion, almost sitting down. "Are you sure?"

"You're welcome to leave him a note."

Just like Jake to make things difficult for her. She stormed back to the desk. "Where's his office?"

"You can't go in his office."

"Fine. When I tell him I was here and that you refused to let me go into my husband's office, you're the one who is going to catch hell."

"Husband?" She looked like she'd just found out her puppy had died. "Jake's not married."

"I'm his best kept secret."

The girl's shoulders sagged, and her jaw dropped. "I'm sorry, Mrs. Adams. It's around the corner. The big office on the left."

Sylvia bulled past her and charged into Jake's office. She glanced around the room. It was nicely furnished, but it needed a few plants. Next time she visited her *husband,* she snickered, she'd bring a potted lily.

She opened her bag and got out a notepad and pen.

Dear Jake. A hard man is good to find...

After she finished writing the note, she ripped it off the pad, folded it, and set it on his desk. She turned to leave, and as she strolled to the door she purred, "Surprise, Jakie-pooh."

***

Jake returned to his office an hour after dusk. His lights were still on. "Who forgot to turn off my lights again?" he muttered. "How many times have I told them..?" Too many long days were taking a toll on his patience.

Eager to unload the mountain of paperwork he had acquired from his meeting with the Major, he entered his office and dropped his heavy satchel beside the desk. As he sat in his leather chair, he noticed a folded note set smack dab in the middle of his blotter. Who would leave him a note? Marianne? A bolt of pleasure rushed through his heart. He opened the note and settled back in his chair.

Dearest Jake, A hard man is good to find. Meet me for lunch tomorrow at Joe Am Ku'damm, 12:30. We need to talk. Don't be late. Love, Sylvia.

A blade of coldblooded dread stabbed Jake in the chest. She was here in Berlin. She had been in his office. What did she tell everyone? Did she cause a scene?

Oh my God. What kind of trouble am I in now?

He wadded the note and flung it across the room. His temples throbbed. He massaged them as nightmarish thoughts from the past terrorized him, her animalist love making that was more like ritualistic mating, her constant nitpicking, bitching, and demanding...God she was a bitch.

What does she want from me this time?

No way would she want to return his money or say she was sorry. More likely she was there to dig her sharp claws into his throat again. And her timing couldn't have been worse.

How am I going to explain her to Marianne?

Oh damn. As hard as he'd tried to avoid telling her about Sylvia, now there was no way around it. The proverbial feces hitting the fan was about to splatter him in the face.

He got up and retrieved the note from the floor and gritted his teeth. The only way to find out why she was here and what she wanted was to meet her for lunch. How much was she going to cost him this time? Her price had to be high. It always was. He could lose Marianne again, this time forever.

***

Jo Am Ku'damm was a chic café along the busy Kurfürstendamm and world famous for the *in-crowd* who frequented it. On warm, sunny days, business folks could enjoy a leisurely lunch at cozy tables along the sidewalk. As Jake approached the café, he spotted Sylvia seated at one of those tables. His heart lurched with dread and banged against his ribcage. Two young men were flirting with her. She could have been a pampered housecat, purring at the attentions of her suitors.

Jake's eyes narrowed as he watched her toy with them. She looked the same as he remembered her, perhaps better; slim legs crossed at the knee, a spiked high-heel dangling from her toes, cigarette pinched between sleek fingers as she blew smoke at the foolish boys. She sported a bewitching smile and wove a sexy aura about her, drawing men to her like bees to honey. The problem was, however, that her kind of honey was tinged with poison.

Her gaze zeroed in on him, as if she'd known he'd been standing on the corner all along. A teasing smile played over her lips, telling him that she was glad he had found her in this state of high demand. She waved off her playthings, and with a flip of her cigarette, gestured for him to join her.

It required every ounce of composure he possessed to maintain a calm expression, though his jaw muscles felt like bear trap springs. He wanted to strangle her, in public, so everyone could see her choke to death on the sidewalk. The thought produced a brittle smile. He pulled out the offered chair and sat down. "What are you doing here?"

"Oh, Jake. Don't be like that," Sylvia cooed and fluttered her long eyelashes. "It's a free world."

"No it isn't."

She examined him from head to toe and purred, "You're looking mighty fine," and dragged on her cigarette.

He felt mentally raped by her brazen inspection. "Compliments will get you nowhere. Haven't you done enough damage—?"

"Now, now, Jake. That's water under the bridge."

He'd like to throw her off a bridge, a tall one, built above a highway with lots of truck traffic.

She reached over and walked her red fingernails up his arm, making his skin crawl under his sleeve. "It appears the Army has been good to you, kept you in prime condition. Yum."

He jerked his arm away. "What do you want, Sylvia?"

A thin eyebrow arched as if he'd hurt her feelings. "I thought you might want to see me again. Just when things were getting interesting between us, you dumped me for another woman."

"Sylvia, we weren't meant to be together."

"Easy for you to say." She crushed out her cigarette in the ash tray and blew her last drag into his face.

He batted at the smoke.

Tapping on the menu lying in front of him, she said, "Pick out what you'd like for lunch. It's my treat." Then she plucked a strawberry from a small dish on the table. "Want one?" She put it to her puckered lips and licked it before she sucked it into her mouth and squished it.

Jake frowned. "It's over between us."

"It's not over until I say it's over."

"Then let's cut to the chase, Sylvia." Drawing the wrinkled note from the inside pocket of his jacket, he flipped it across the table at her. "Why did you come to Berlin?"

She glanced at the paper. "Weren't you happy I left you a note?"

"I'd be happier if you were here to give me back my money."

She laughed. "That'll never happen, Jake. Consider it payment for my sexual services."

A waitress stepped up to their table. "Have you decided?" she asked in German.

Sylvia snapped her menu closed. "I'd like a slice of cheesecake and a glass of burgundy wine." Glancing at Jake, she asked in a breathless voice, "What are you having, *dear*?"

Jake flinched at the word *dear*. The tone she used made it sound dirty. "I'm not hungry."

The waitress curtseyed, picked up their menus, and dashed back into the café.

Sylvia's expression turned droopy-eyed dejected. "Won't you at least have some coffee?"

"I'm not thirsty."

"Don't be angry," she cooed. "I'm here on vacation and I happened to find out you were stationed here. I don't want any trouble, really." She painted on a sweet smile and batted her eyelashes.

What a liar. "You said we had to talk." He indicated the note as evidence. "Talk about what?"

A sommelier delivered a fresh glass of wine and bowed. "Madam —"

"Buzz off."

He left.

Sylvia reached out and placed her hand on Jake's.

His muscles tried to recoil, as if from a hot burner, but he forced his hand to remain still on the table. He had to get her to fess up about what she was after. "Quit stalling. What do you want to talk about, Sylvia?"

Leaning toward him, her eyes glistened as she breathed the word, "Guess."

Okay. He'd play her stupid game. "It's obviously not about my money, so how about you framing me? Maybe you want to tell me how you did it?"

"I have friends in high places. Guess again."

"Maybe you want to tell me what you did with the company's money."

"Guess again."

"How about why you made me miss my wedding?"

"You're getting warmer." She grinned and chucked another strawberry.

Jake's stomach turned, but he had to control his revulsion. "So you want to talk about Marianne?"

"Bingo." She brushed her cheek with the back of her fingers. "That bitch stole you away from me, and now I want you back, Jake."

He almost spit out a laugh in her face. "After what you did to me, not if you were the last woman on earth."

"Now don't be cross." She plastered a phony

pout on her lips. "So what if you had to spend a little time away in that prison place. It gave you a chance to think about what a big mistake you were about to make. I saved you from marrying that girl, kept her from spending all your money. You should be thanking me, buster."

Jake bristled at her flippant remarks. "I was in love with her."

"No. You were in love with me. She poisoned you against me."

"She doesn't even know about you, Sylvia, and I didn't love you."

"You will love me," she growled under her breath. "Things will go back to the way they were before she ruined my life. And you will marry me. I'll be Mrs. Jake Adams, and we are going to live happily ever after. You got that?"

He huffed. "And if I tell you to go to hell?"

She leered at him. "I wouldn't advise that."

"You're full of hot air, that's all."

"Am I now?" She reached in her bag and pulled out a photograph, which she set on the table in front of him. "Now it's my turn to guess."

Jake stared at a picture of him on a dim rooftop, embracing Marianne. Her face wasn't visible. He remembered chasing the photographer. A hot wave of anger crashed over him. Vile words stuck in his throat.

"My guess is...that's Marianne," Sylvia said.

"Who took this picture?" Jake managed. He felt violated down to his core. "You had someone spy on us?"

"Ooh, I'm getting hotter."

Anger turned to terror. Would Sylvia resort to murdering Marianne? "Don't you go anywhere near her."

"Bingo." Sylvia regarded him from under canted brows. "You wouldn't want her to get hurt, now would you?"

"Of course not."

"So you see. We are meant to be together, after all."

"Like hell." He grabbed her glass and tossed the wine down the front of her dress.

She leaped up and fell back, tipping over the table. Strawberries flew everywhere. The dish shattered. The ashtray shattered. The chair toppled over. Standing there aghast, she clutched her breasts in wide-eyed embarrassment, sputtering for words. "You. You! You asshole. How dare you?"

By now, Jake was out of his seat and standing nose to nose with Sylvia. "You stay away from Marianne, you hear?"

Screeching at the top of her lungs, she pulled her hair and screamed, "You'll pay for this, Jake. You just wait and see." She whirled around and stormed toward the taxi stand.

He flipped her the finger. "And you better give me my money back, bitch."

Chapter THIRTEEN

THE NEXT DAY, Sylvia paced her room. She wore a touch of makeup and chose a demure dress for her new mission to locate Jake's beloved Marianne. She'd guessed right; that was the woman in the picture, but the idiotic investigator had failed to capture her face in his photos. However, he had discovered Jake's address and included it in the report. Perhaps something in his apartment would reveal Marianne's whereabouts.

She easily located the apartment in a sprawling complex complete with courtyards and gardens. Getting inside would be another matter. The door was locked, and she had no key.

Whistling drew her attention to a nearby garden. There, an elderly man bent over, transplanting pansies from containers to fresh turned soil. Maybe he worked here and could open the door with some kind of master key.

"Oh, yoo-hoo." She waved a lace handkerchief at him. "*Allo.* Can you please help me? *Cannst mich hiilfen.*"

That got his attention. He slowly stood up, groaning and arching his back as if it ached. Looking her direction, he wiped his sweaty brow with his sleeve, and then slapped dirt from his hands on his pants.

Sylvia ran to him, slightly out of breath. "English? Do you speak English?"

"Yes," he said in a clear tone. "How may I help you?"

Being married to Jake had opened doors for her already, so she spun the lie again. "I'm Jake Adam's wife from the States."

"I'm his landlord. I didn't know Jake was married."

"I'm his best kept secret, but that's going to change."

His blank stare told her he was oblivious to what that meant.

"I just locked myself out of our apartment."

He laughed at her predicament.

"It's not funny. I can't sit outside all day waiting for him to get off work. I've got dishes to wash and laundry to clean, and if supper isn't ready when he gets home, well, I don't have to tell you how much trouble I'd be in. Besides—"

"All right, all right, Mrs. Adams. I understand." He dug a key out of his pocket. "I'm pretty busy right now." He indicated his planting project and then handed her the key. "Let yourself in and drop this back at the office as soon as you can."

"Thank you, sir."

"Be more careful next time."

"I will. I promise." She ran back to Jake's locked door, thinking that was too easy.

Once inside, she hurried through his apartment,

searching for anything that might lead her to Marianne. Conflicting emotions needled her. On one hand, she was thrilled to have found Jake again. On the other, she was irritated that he managed to beat the bum embezzlement rap, after which she'd lost track of him.

At least he's still single. Feisty, but single.

He would warm up to her soon. He just needed some encouragement, a little motivation.

And when he finds out how serious I am about using Marianne for that motivation, he'll leap into my arms.

In his bedroom, she rummaged through his dresser. No bras and panties, meaning she didn't live here. The closet held only his clothes and fresh uniforms all nicely pressed. She made a mental note to remind him that she didn't do ironing, or cooking for that matter.

At the desk, she examined every scrap of paper for an address, an envelope, anything of Marianne's, but came up empty. Maybe *she* was *his* best kept secret.

In the living room, she plopped down on the sofa and cradled her head in her hands. The silent loneliness of Jake's empty home was heartbreaking. Bare walls, plastic plants, a cinder block and plywood bookcase lined with spine-cracked paperbacks and ragged stacks of hardcovers. No television, radio. Jake was a broken man. He needed her more than ever. There had to be some way to convince him that she was much better for him than Marianne.

There just has to be something around here.

She glanced across the coffee table and spied a book underneath some magazines. It was appointment book. She thumbed through the pages. No Marianne in the address section. However, the day-planner calendar revealed a notation: *Marianne over to cook dinner. 2pm*

"Hmmm…" Sylvia caught her breath, and her thoughts turned black. She recalled how close she'd cut it that day, getting Jake arrested just an hour before his wedding. Then she'd used a credit card to open the door to the apartment he shared with his waiting bride. Sylvia then absconded with his belongings to make it look like he'd moved out. Through her connections at the police department, whom she'd regularly recruited with sexual favors, she managed to delay Jake's one phone call until the following Monday, long after the wedding was ruined and Marianne became a jilted bride. That would teach her to steal another woman's man.

But somehow they'd gotten back together again, here in Berlin, a city of three million people, like finding the proverbial needle in a haystack. She tapped a long fingernail on her chin, thinking she might need the investigator's help to locate Marianne. The thought of seeing that disgusting man again made her shudder, but he did a decent job and he kept his mouth shut, though he was a lousy photographer.

That made her think about Jake and photographs. What kind of man had a girlfriend but no pictures of her, no love letters, nothing…? Unless he kept them in a book.

She got off the couch and rushed to the makeshift bookshelves. On top of the hard cover books lay a photo album. Excitement lit fires in her bloodstream as she opened the book and discovered a picture of Jake and a woman. She was a cute woman, long hair, she looked about four inches shorter than Jake. The background suggested the picture was taken on a boat, blue sky, white railings, gulls fluttering overhead. But there was something familiar about this woman's face. On closer inspection, she was startled to recognize the woman from the American Consulate who had helped her get a new passport.

"Hello, Marianne." Sylvia cackled.

No need to hire that weasel of an investigator now.

Chapter FOURTEEN

O NE DAY WHILE JAKE was out of town on military business with the Major, Heinrich called Marianne's office. "If you are free, I'd like to take you to lunch today."

Marianne thought it would be nice to catch up with her friend. "I'd like that. Is 11:30 okay with you?"

"Perfect." Heinrich sounded pleased. "I'll pick you up in front of the Consulate. See you then."

At 11:25, she stepped outside and noticed a cream-colored Mercedes in the parking lot. The horn tooted once, and Heinrich leaped out of the car to open the passenger door. "You look lovely today." His eyes trailed over her, admiring her smart suit jacket and short skirt.

Marianne enjoyed Heinrich's taste in clothes, and today he wore a nice pair of brown corduroy slacks, a green shirt, and a German hat, complete with feathers and colorful pins. "My, my, Heinrich, don't you look outdoorsy today?"

"*Danke*." He started the car and drove away from the Consulate.

"Your pins." Marianne pointed to his hat. "What are those about?"

"Ah, yes. The pins." Heinrich chuckled.

"Throughout the year I participate in several *volksmarches* or group hikes, and for every one that I complete, I obtain a pin for my hat. I also collect them when I travel throughout Europe."

Marianne grinned. "Perhaps we can do one together sometime. I love to hike."

"Yes, perhaps." Heinrich glanced at her and added, "very soon, I hope," and then pulled in front of a little café only a few blocks from the Consulate.

The Café Vienna was a tiny establishment, very plain with no fancy decorations, yet filled with the wonderful aroma of home cooking. Marianne's mouth watered as Heinrich guided her to an empty table by a street-side window.

She studied her surroundings. Just outside the window, a variety of flowers flourished in a planter box. Inside, there were lots of dark-wood tables and chairs, very *old-worldly*, along with the din of light conversation and soft music. She felt comfortable.

A waitress handed her a menu. The offerings reminded her of her grandmother's cooking, comfort food, rich pork, ham, veal, dumplings, gravy, the kind of fare that doctors warned everyone against eating. Marianne saw what she wanted to order. "I'd like a big bowl of Schnecken soup, please," she told the waitress.

Heinrich closed his menu and placed his order. "*Ein Wienerschnitzel, bitte.*"

Once the waitress left, Heinrich reached across the table and took Marianne's hand. "It's so good to see you again. Are you settling into your job and your new life here?"

"It's had its ups and downs."

His eyes were as warm and inviting as his smile. "Berlin certainly agrees with you."

She felt flushed under his praise and lucky to have found a friend as nice as Heinrich. He was attractive, as well, which made her feel a little awkward and a bit conflicted in her feelings for him, especially when he reached his free hand across the table and took her other hand. Holding both his hands like this didn't seem right. Seemed more like the way a bride and groom would stand in front of each other as they pronounced their undying love and devotion for each other.

Thankfully, the waitress brought the soup. Marianne's stomach growled. The rising steam smelled wonderful.

Heinrich released her hands.

She dug in with her spoon and noticed his eyes glitter in amusement. After she ate a couple spoonfuls of soup, he chuckled. And after downing the fourth spoonful, she could no longer stand not knowing what he found so amusing. "What's so funny?"

"How is your soup?"

"It's a little salty for ham."

Heinrich chuckled. "You didn't order Schinkin soup."

She looked into her bowl. "It's not ham soup?"

"You ordered Schnecken soup. Snails."

"Uggh." Her tongue felt like it was growing a coat of fur. "Snail soup?"

Heinrich laughed. "I didn't know you liked snails so much."

"I don't." She pushed the bowl away, her once growling stomach now turning over. "My German language skills need a little fine tuning."

"You're welcome to have some of my lunch," he said. "Unless you'd rather order something different."

She didn't have time to order another meal. "What have you got there?"

"Breaded veal. It's really very good." He asked the waitress for a separate plate, and once she brought it, he cut his portion in half and scooped it onto the new plate. "This will be much better than snails."

Marianne dove in.

Heinrich scooted his chair closer to her.

Somewhere in the back of her mind, a warning bell rang.

"Much better, eh?" Heinrich asked as he looped his arm around her shoulders. "I am pleased that we are such good friends."

She froze.

What's he doing?

Then over the din she heard the familiar snap of a camera shutter. A quick scan of the room revealed a tourist taking a snapshot of a woman, his wife maybe, but the angle put Heinrich and her in the background. The fiasco on the rooftop had made her extra sensitive about people taking pictures.

"Something wrong?" he asked.

Marianne looked at him, confused at his change

in behavior. She opened her mouth to ask him why, but he suddenly leaned in and kissed her on the lips.

In that split second, the tourist's camera shutter snapped again.

Marianne yanked her head back, leaving Heinrich's mouth frozen in mid-kiss.

"What the hell do you think you're doing?" she demanded.

"But Marianne—"

She pushed him back and leaped up out of her chair. "I thought we were friends?"

"I...uh," he stuttered. "I'm sorry, Marianne. We *are* friends. For a moment, though, I thought we could be more than just friends."

"You thought wrong."

"Please forgive me."

Everyone in the café was watching her. Embarrassment set in like the plague. She spun around and rushed out of the café. Once on the street, tremors rocked her body as hot tears flooded her eyes.

She felt like a good friend had just died.

Chapter FIFTEEN

THE NEXT DAY, Jake was on his way to have lunch with Marianne. He didn't look forward to explaining Sylvia to her. He'd been walking a thin line regarding his past, but just how and where and when to tell her was a challenge. With Sylvia in town, this made it even more challenging, and more urgent.

He clenched his jaw. What if Sylvia found Marianne first? What would Sylvia say to her? What would Sylvia do to her? He shivered as worse-case scenarios came to mind, a knife, a gun, and a pack of lies.

He'd better tell her today and get it over with. It could be a matter of life and death.

As he approached the heavy glass and iron entrance to the American Consulate, a deliveryman was at the door, attempting to juggle an oversized bouquet of flowers while pawing for the door handle.

Jake jogged up to the struggling man and opened the door wide for him.

"*Danke,*" the man said and wriggled carefully through the doorway, stepping sideways as if mindful not to crush a single pedal on the bouquet.

Once inside, Jake followed the deliveryman through security and across the main lobby to the stairs. They were both headed in the same direction. And when he pushed through the glass doors of the passport lobby, Jake wondered who the lucky girl was getting the flowers. Birthday, anniversary, somebody was going to have a good day.

The man walked up to Carla. "I have a delivery for Marianne Tucker."

Jake's heart dropped to the bottom of his stomach like a rock down a well. Who had sent Marianne flowers? The bouquet was enormous. Whoever he was wanted to make a grand statement.

"Marianne is in a meeting at the moment and cannot be disturbed." Carla gleamed at the flowers, and then gave a quick you-have-competition nod toward Jake. "I'll be happy to give these to Marianne once she's free."

The deliveryman smiled. "Great. I appreciate that." As he whirled around, he added, "Have a nice day."

Jake watched Carla heft the mountain of flowers and take them into Marianne's office. When Carla returned, he asked, "Who were those from?"

Carla responded, "Heinrich. He's just a friend." She smiled slyly.

Jake saw that look again. Was she trying to tell him something? Based on the expensive flowers and the silent messages from Carla, perhaps Marianne's relationship with Heinrich was more than *just friends*.

And where were they going with it? Courtship? Engagement? Marriage?

Jake's stomach churned. Just when he was about

to tell her about Sylvia and come clean, now it looked as if he had some serious competition. His mind clouded with doubt. He didn't want to get in the middle of Marianne's affair with Heinrich. Maybe she would be happier with him. At least that guy didn't have a crazed psycho-bitch in his closet. And if what Jake suspected was true, he loved her enough to set her free so she could be happy.

His heart ached at the thought of losing her again. Maybe that was best for her. Hot tears stung his eyes. He turned around and quickly exited the lobby before anyone could see those tears spill down his cheeks.

***

Marianne finished her conference call and stepped out to ask Carla if she'd seen Jake. It was time he arrived for lunch, and she was hungry. But since Carla was nowhere to be found, she shrugged and walked into her office. She saw a huge bouquet of flowers on her desk. They were a magnificent collection of gladiolas, daises, dahlias, foxglove, and white roses.

"Oh, my, how beautiful." She saw the attached note addressed to her and thought it was from Jake. "He is so sweet."

Marianne...

I was a fool the way I acted toward you at lunch yesterday. Please forgive me. It will never happen again. I respect your desire for us to remain friends. Please call me when we can be friends again. Heinrich.

He concluded with his phone number.

That was thoughtful of him to apologize, but she didn't want to play courtship games with Heinrich, if that was what he was doing. She felt more inclined to concentrate on rekindling her relationship with Jake and didn't want any complications from other suitors.

She heard the copier chugging in the backroom and walked in to find Carla busy copying a stack of papers.

"Have you seen Jake?"

"Yep. He was here when the flowers arrived."

"Oh no." Marianne felt a sense of impending doom.

"And not only did he see the flowers, I told him they were from Heinrich. That's when he left, in a bit of a hurry, I believe."

"Why would you do such a thing?" Marianne's face heated with anger. "You had no right."

"Come on, Marianne. A little competition is a good thing for Jake. You guys have been running hot and cold. Heinrich could be the catalyst to get you two together, or for you to realize your relationship with Jake is not going to work."

"But you gave him the wrong impression. I'm *not* in a relationship with Heinrich, so there is no competition." She looked toward the glass lobby doors. Maybe she could still catch him. "He just left?"

"No. He's long gone."

Irritation began to replace her former sense of doom.

So Jake thinks I'm in a relationship with Heinrich,

and what does he do? He tucks his tail between his legs and runs away.

"Men. I'm done with them." She stormed back to her office and slammed her door.

***

Later that evening, Marianne began to prepare dinner at her apartment. Shortly after locating some left-over spaghetti at the back of the refrigerator, the phone rang.

"Hello, Marianne." Jake's voice sounded distant.

She experienced a flood of mixed emotions: she was furious that he didn't stick around to take her to lunch, maybe because he was jealous of Heinrich, or perhaps his feelings were hurt over the flowers. Worse, this wasn't the first time he was a *no-show*.

"Hello?" Jake said, breaking her muse.

"What's going on with you, Jake? You stood me up for lunch."

"I stopped by your office—"

"And saw the flowers, I know, and bigmouth Carla told you they were from Heinrich."

Jake didn't say anything right away, and then, "You and Heinrich must be getting along well. Have you been seeing a lot of him lately?" His tone was better suited for his death bed.

"Are you jealous?"

"I'm hurt and confused, Marianne. I need to know, I should step aside so you and Heinrich can—"

"Stop it, Jake." Marianne rolled her eyes. "Heinrich and I are just friends. Friends. Do you hear me?"

His response was silence.

"Are you still there?"

She heard him suck in a breath. "So what were the flowers all about?"

"Heinrich made an ass out of himself the other day. The flowers were an apology. But if you think to buy me flowers to make up for your asinine behavior, don't bother."

"What did he do?"

"That's none of your business."

"Okay, I get it. But I still want to know so I don't make the same mistake."

"You didn't show up for lunch. That's worse than what Heinrich did. Why didn't you stay and ask me about the flowers? I would have told you, and we could have had a nice lunch, but you assumed the worse and gave up on me so easily."

"I thought I'd already lost you."

"Ever hear of fighting for someone you love?"

A moment passed before Jake responded. "You have every right to be mad."

"I'm not mad. I'm disappointed in you, Jake."

"That's worse. If you're mad you could slap my face and get over it, but disappointed, well, I have to change my behavior to fix that."

"Am I not worth it?"

"Okay, then. I'll fight for you, if that's what you want."

"It's not about what I want. It's about you, Jake. You've got to want to fight for me, at least ask me about what's bothering you before you run off."

"I will. I promise."

"And it goes both ways, Jake. Something is bothering me. I've asked you about it, but you're not being honest with me. I want to know why you joined the Army."

"All right. Let's talk about it at lunch. My calendar is jammed this week, how about next Monday."

"You're stalling, Jake."

"I can't help it. The Major is dragging me to meetings all over Europe. They're talking about the future of the Berlin Wall."

Marianne blinked. That sounded like a good reason.

"We'll go to the café down the street from the Consulate. Okay?"

That was the same café Heinrich had taken her to lunch and took liberties with his lips. Wouldn't that be the pits if she and Jake ran into him there?

"Okay, I'll wait until Monday." Marianne placed the phone on the hook and shook her head. He'd better clear things up then, or love wouldn't be in their future, after all.

Chapter SIXTEEN

IT WAS MONDAY, and a summer breeze fluttered the frill around the green umbrella that sheltered Jake and Marianne's table. Jasmine blossoms scented the air, and bees buzzed from flower to flower in the window planter boxes. Heinrich hadn't made an appearance.

She had just finished lunch when Jake lifted his wine glass to her in a toast. "To you, the woman of my dreams." Jake's eyes glittered, and then he took a sip.

In spite of his procrastinating, she never imagined a few months ago that she'd enjoy his company, let alone be falling in love with him again. Still, there was that elephant in the room, the unrevealed truth about why he joined the Army. "You have something to tell me, Jake."

He cleared his throat. "I've got a better idea. How about if I take you away from all this?"

"What do you mean…all this?"

Jake cocked one eyebrow and spoke like a Frenchman with a thick accent. "Mon Cheri, it would give me great pleasure if I could whisk you away and have you to myself for a whole weekend." Then placing his hand over his heart, he looked skyward as he continued his comic routine. "Imagine just you and me dancing underneath the stars, making our own music, the music of love."

Under normal circumstances, she might have laughed and joined in with something like, "Oh, kind sir, where do you plan on whisking me away to? New York, Paris, London?" but she decided to keep him on track. "Where do you want to take me, Jake?"

Returning to his natural voice, he replied, "Goslar."

She'd never heard of the place. "Where's Goslar?"

"It's in West Germany. I hear the inn has a romantic indoor pool, great food, and..." he added with a provocative wink, "soft feather beds."

She had feared that this subject of a sleepover would eventually come up, so she was prepared with an answer. "Jake, you know we've talked about taking things slow."

He nodded. "So?"

"Just when everything is going right between us, I don't want things to be ruined because we jumped into bed together."

With eyes widening in genuine surprise, he asked, "Ruin things? What could be more romantic than going away for the weekend, just the two of us?"

"It goes beyond romance, Jake, and you know it."

He straightened in his chair. "I thought you might like to go. Besides, I want us to have time together so I can answer all your questions."

She had to get back to work, so anything he had

to say now would be rushed. Perhaps time away from their daily routine would be a good idea. "I'll go with you on two conditions."

He groaned. "What conditions?"

"Number one, I help pay the expenses. And number two, we don't fool around."

"You mean no sex?"

He knew full well what she meant, but he obviously wanted her to spell it out. "Right. No sex."

"How about necking and some heavy petting?" He grinned.

"You've been out of my life for a long time and suddenly we're back together again. It's all happening way too fast. Besides, up to now you haven't been totally honest with me and that plays a big part in my feeling this way."

"I'm working on that."

She reached over and took his hand. "Jake, if we're really meant to be together, sex will happen in its own time. Why rush things before I'm satisfied that you're not going to crush my heart again. And in the meantime, we should get to know each other again."

"Okay, Marianne. No sex. But I don't want you to help out with the expenses. Call me old-fashioned, I guess, but it's my treat." He gave her a lopsided grin.

"All right, Old-Fashioned. When are we going?"

"Next weekend all right with you?"

"I'll have to check my schedule—"

"Don't give me that. You know you're free as a

bird."

"And you know I can't sound too eager."

"Then it's settled. I'll take care of all the paperwork to get us through the Berlin Corridor. We'll leave Friday afternoon."

"That's all fine and dandy, Jake, but get this. I'm fed up with your stalling. While we're in Goslar, if you don't tell me the real reason why you ran off and joined the Army, you and I are through."

And she meant it.

***

Marianne's excitement grew with each passing day. She felt happy that Jake was finally willing to answer her questions and hopeful that he would tell the truth and not leave anything out.

However, she had heard plenty of stories about traveling by car through the infamous Berlin Corridor, the road that connected West Berlin to West Germany. Leaving the safety of West Berlin was risky. For any reason, or no reason at all, they could be detained by East German authorities.

She shuddered at the thought of being stuck in a jail cell in a communist country. At least Jake had made this trip before, so she trusted him to stay out of trouble. They would drive a maze of highways through 110 miles of East Germany and deal face-to-face with armed Russian guards and East German Police at several checkpoints along the way. She felt apprehensive, but Jake had told her all she had to do was stay in the car at each checkpoint and let him deal with the authorities. Once they got through the final checkpoint, the journey would be much easier.

In spite of the dangers and uncertainties, she was looking forward to this trip.

Friday afternoon came quickly, and Jake arrived in his Porsche on time to pick her up at her apartment. He wore jeans and a pressed shirt, tennis shoes and no socks. As he pushed her suitcase into the trunk, which was in the front, he said, "I've packed a lunch and something to drink in a bag behind the seat, in case we get hungry." He shut the lid.

She got in and buckled up. He did the same and peeled away from the curb.

Within a few minutes, they arrived at the West Berlin border. Trucks, buses, and cars jammed the traffic lanes. Jake got out and disappeared into a large building. After a few minutes, he returned to the car with a slim black book. Flipping it open, he showed her a sequence of photographs of the road signs they were supposed to watch for along the way.

"Our instructions are very clear." He spoke in a serious tone. "And we must follow them precisely. As long as we are in the Corridor, we cannot stop for any reason. And you, my dear, are the navigator. As we drive, you will look at the book and the road signs and the map and ensure that I am on the right road."

"I thought you did this trip before?"

"I wasn't driving."

She felt a rush of panic. "How do I know what road signs are correct?"

He handed her the book and pointed to the first page. "It will be easy. Here, see this?" He tapped the first photograph. "This is the first sign. Now look at the words below. It tells you how many kilometers we need to go before we see the next sign. It's on the next page." He turned the page, which displayed another highway sign. "Just match up the signs and we'll be fine."

"Looks easy enough." She felt a little more confident now that she had an idea of what to expect.

And so the journey began.

She enjoyed the intrigue of the Corridor. At each checkpoint, they waited in a long line of traffic and inched to the gate. Jake saluted the border guard who would then walk around the car in a cursory check for God knew what. How many defecting East German citizens could be hidden in a Porsche? And then he would motion Jake to proceed.

The car seemed small compared to the multitude of trucks, both military and civilian, convoying through the Corridor and clogging up the highways. Jake kept pace with the traffic flow instead of passing everyone.

She felt a shiver of dread each time she saw East German guards peering at them through binoculars from their guard towers along the way. And patrolling the highway, square East German cars called *Trabants* would drive up alongside them, and the armed guards inside would give them the once over.

Many times she caught Jake giving her the once

over, as well. He had this sly tweak to his smile that made her think he was happy she had agreed to go on this trip with him. If he thought there was some gratitude coming his way tonight, in the form of kisses and sex, he had another think coming. Engrossed in her musings, she forgot her duty as navigator. But she didn't forget her stomach or the lunch he'd packed. They'd been on the road an hour.

"Want a sandwich?" she asked him as she reached over the seatback for the lunch bag.

"Sure."

She fiddled with the jackets, but couldn't find their lunch, even in this cramped space. "Where is it?"

He turned to help her, momentarily taking his eyes off the road, and reached back to move a blanket. "Right here."

When he turned back to the road, he shouted, "Crap. We just blew by the exit." He cranked the steering wheel to the right shoulder, stopped, and peered at the rear view mirror.

"What are you doing?" Her chest filled with hot alarm.

"You're supposed to be watching for that turn."

"I'm sorry. I was hungry. What's wrong with your eyes?"

"I just caught a glimpse of the sign as we passed it."

"No big deal. Turn around at the next exchange and go back."

Jake looked pale with concern. "We're going to get arrested, I just know it."

"Arrested?" She wasn't hungry anymore. "It was an honest mistake."

"Since I'm in Army Intelligence, the communists would love an excuse to arrest us as spies."

"Spies? Oh my God."

Jake's eyes grew determined.

A delivery truck sped by. He gunned the gas and whipped a u-turn, going east in the westbound lane. Oncoming trucks hugged the right shoulder, honked and flashed their lights.

"Jake, what the hell?"

"We can't waste any more time. The authorities clock our progress from checkpoint to checkpoint. If we arrive late, we can be detained for questioning."

"Damned if we do, damned if we don't."

"This is not a free country. Many innocent people never see the light of day."

Anger shot through her like a bullet. "How could you put me in this kind of danger?"

"I didn't think we'd miss a turnoff."

"I knew I shouldn't have come."

"We're not busted yet." His jaw muscles twitched as he approached the exit ramp they'd missed.

Ahead, she saw a break in the traffic small enough to squeak a roller skate through. She braced herself against the dash. "Jake!"

"Hang on." He executed a tire-squealing left turn, shot the gap between the oncoming trucks, and fishtailed up the exit ramp. Blaring horns faded behind them. "See? Piece of cake."

She saw red. If looks could kill, Jake would have been choking himself to death. She beat on his shoulder with a fist. "You ever do that to me again...God damn it, Jake." Hot tears blurred her vision. "You scared the hell out of me."

"We're not out of the woods yet."

"What are you talking about? We're back on course, right?"

"I hope nobody reports us. Meanwhile, keep your eyes on the map."

"Keep your own eyes on the map."

"Okay. I'm sorry." He patted her thigh. "But you've got to admit, that was fun." And he laughed.

She held her breath and the words that could berate him all the way to Goslar. Just one look at the smile on his face, she knew she couldn't stay angry at him for long.

***

An hour later, the car approached the far end of the corridor: the gateway to West Germany. Although Jake had traveled the route once before as a passenger in a military convoy, he feared a flat tire or some other complication might have made him arrive late and give the East German guards cause to detain him. He hoped he'd made up the lost time the missed ramp had caused, but not by too much. Get there too soon and the guards would ticket him for speeding.

One of his biggest concerns centered on his Military Intelligence status and his close connection to 766MID, of which the East Germans and Russians were aware. They would look for any excuse to detain him, but since driving was the most convenient form of transportation in West Germany, he had to put up with any harassment so he'd have a car to get around in. If he had flown or took the overnight Duty Train, he would have had to find a rental car, and the rates were astronomical.

Jake relaxed once he got through the East German checkpoint and entered the American checkpoint. He parked in front of the building. Marianne rushed off to the ladies room.

Inside, an MP saluted him and checked his papers. "Any trouble on the road, sir?"

If a report about his wild driving had been filed, an APB would have been posted for his car, and the East German's would have locked him up by now. "Smooth sailing, sarge."

"Where are you headed?"

"Goslar."

"Ah, the Imperial City of West Germany. Very romantic."

"A guy can hope."

The sergeant smiled, stamped Jake's papers, and handed them back. "Have a safe trip, sir." He executed a quick salute.

"Thanks." Jake returned the salute, left the building, and strolled back to the car. Marianne had returned, hair freshly brushed and new lipstick in place.

He settled in behind the wheel. "That's all taken care of."

"Thanks for getting us here safely."

"My pleasure. Now we're ready for a weekend of fun."

The late afternoon sun was still high enough to give him a perfect view of the rolling green hills, accented with splashes of yellow flowers. Jake entwined his fingers with Marianne's as she scanned the windmills that dotted the landscape.

"This is beautiful."

"Hard to imagine this scene marred by war."

He slowed the car and wound through a village of dark red brick and timber.

"Jake, stop. I must take a picture of this."

He stepped on the brakes and stopped the car along the roadside. "What is it?"

She grabbed her camera from behind the seat, threw open the door, and leaped out of the car. Passing traffic whizzed by. She snapped a picture of a plump old woman wearing a tattered dress and scarf, riding an old bicycle toward her. It was laden with three squawking geese in a wire basket hooked on the handlebars. Marianne squealed with delight.

Jake shook his head and smiled.

Now this is the Marianne I remember.

"Come on, let's go. We're almost there."

She scrambled back into her seat. "I'm going to frame that one." And closed the door.

"Good for you." Within a few minutes, he drove into the town of Goslar and turned into the hotel's parking lot. The hotel was an ancient stone building, two stories tall with lots of windows.

Bags in hand, he led Marianne to the front desk.

An elderly clerk looked up from his book and greeted them. "*Guten Abend.*"

"We have a reservation for two nights," Jake announced in English.

The clerk's puffy eyes danced with cheer as he grinned at them. "Your name?"

"Mr. and Mrs. Jake Adams," he replied without hesitation.

"Jake." She swatted his arm.

He hoped she'd get used to hearing that pretty soon.

As the clerk checked their names on the list, Jake noticed Marianne roll her eyes. She didn't say another word. Her tight-lipped smile, however, sent the message: *we will talk about this very soon, Jake.*

"Your room is upstairs," the clerk said, holding out a single key.

"One room?" Marianne piped up. "We needed two rooms. There must be some mistake."

The clerk looked at her like she'd grown another nose. "There is only one room, I'm afraid."

Hoping to defuse the situation, Jake jumped in with, "Apparently there was a misunderstanding when I made the reservation. My German's not that good, as you know. It's not his fault."

"Then there had better be two beds in that room, or you're sleeping in the hallway."

"Fine." He took the key from the clerk and struggled up the narrow wooden stairs, juggling bags. Once he found the door, he turned the key in the lock and pushed his way in. Two queen beds. He was in luck.

Marianne peeked inside the room. "Did you plan this all along?"

"No, of course not."

"I told you no sex."

"And I respect that." He tossed the bags on the nearest bed. "I'll take this one."

After a quick unpacking job, he led her to the window where an evening breeze fluttered the curtains. The scene could have come straight out of a Hansel and Gretel fairytale. Bicyclists peddled down bumpy cobblestone streets edged with wood and brick buildings, freshly painted, it seemed, and heavy on the wooden trim. Flower boxes hung from almost every windowsill, and strains of accordion music filtered in from a pub down the way. The air felt rich and thick with the aromas of grilled bratwurst and baked bread.

He gave in to a wave of tenderness and gathered Marianne in his arms. He wanted to love her, to protect her always, and nuzzling the top of her head, he inhaled her fragrance.

She smells wonderful.

She seemed to relax in his arms and laid her head against his chest. Birds sang to each other in the distance, calling their mates to roost. He wanted to lift her in his arms and take her to the bed, their roost, but he knew better than to even try that stunt. "Let's get some dinner."

He followed the enticing aroma down the stairs

to the hotel's restaurant where he treated her to a hearty dinner while listening to a lively band. Soon afterwards, he took her outside, led her hand-in-hand along cobblestone walkways, and marveled at the German architecture, which was breathtaking at every turn.

"Feel like being spoiled tonight?" He squeezed her hand.

"Sure, why not?"

He escorted her to an old building with filtered light pouring out from under elegant arches and led her inside. "You won't need this." He lifted her shawl from her shoulders and draped it on a nearby coat hook.

She must have suddenly realized that they were in a café. "We're eating again?" she asked. "I couldn't eat another bite."

He laughed. "I think you might find this tempting."

After seating her at a small table for two, which was covered with white linen, he pointed to a small button mounted at the end of the table.

"Watch this." Exaggerating a pompous attitude, he pressed the button. A faint buzzing noise brought a smiling waiter in a black tuxedo and bowtie out to greet them. Without speaking, he handed them both over-sized menus, bowed, spun around, and disappeared into the backroom.

Answering Marianne's quizzical look of *How do you know about this place*, Jake explained, "A friend of mine told me about the buzzers. But the most important thing you need to know is that they have the best desserts in Germany."

She groaned then eyed the dessert menu.

He stared at her, wishing he didn't have to ruin this beautiful weekend by telling her about Sylvia.

After a moment, she looked up, and he looked down, fearing she'd caught him staring. She smiled and pointed to the button. "If you're ready, I'd like to do the honors this time."

"By all means, my dear, be my guest." Jake waved his hand toward the button.

She pushed it. A faint buzz, and within seconds, the tuxedo-clad waiter appeared. "What is your preference, madam?"

"I'll have the chocolate mousse."

"Good choice, and for you, sir?"

"The fruit and cream supreme, please."

"With whipped topping and sprinkles?"

"Of course, thank you."

The waiter was off.

Marianne turned her attention to their surroundings, and with amazement aglow in her eyes, she scanned the beautiful arched ceilings and the walls adorned with colorful painted scenes of the town. Glittering crystal chandeliers hung from the vaulted ceiling, and golden chains crisscrossed the room. Hand carved figurines depicting German folktale characters stood in every little nook and cranny.

She reached across the table and took Jake's hand. The gesture surprised him, but not as much as the loving look in her eyes. A gentle smile played on her lips as she scooted her chair closer to his side. "Is this where you tell me why you ran off and joined the Army?"

He swallowed hard. Everything was going so smoothly. "Can it wait? I mean, why ruin this beautiful evening?"

"So what you have to tell me...is that going to change things between us?"

"The past always screws up the present, at least for us." He glanced at the backroom door and wished the desserts would appear and get him out of this conversation.

"Tell me now, Jake, or I'll take the train back to Berlin, walk if I have to, and everything about us will be in the past...forever."

"You wouldn't."

"Who framed you?"

A non-answer meant she would leave him sitting here like a frog on a toadstool. It seemed like she was going to push the issue even if it meant they'd both drown in the pond. "All right." He grabbed a breath, more for courage than any other reason. "There's someone I haven't told you about...a woman."

She tweaked her brows. "Woman? A mistress?"

"No, a girlfriend, before us."

"Come on, Jake. What's she got to do with the Army?"

He swallowed. Marianne hadn't walked out yet, so he pressed on. "Her name was Sylvia. I was in a pretty serious relationship with her when you and I met."

"Why didn't you tell me about her then?"

"I didn't want you to know that she blamed you for our breakup."

"Me?"

"I dumped her so I could date you. She thought you stole me from her, so she ruined our wedding."

Marianne sat back in her chair, eyes fixed in a blank stare. "Hell hath no fury like a woman scorned."

"We worked together at the investment firm. She made my days a living hell. And when word went around the office that you and I were getting married, she didn't say another word to me."

"Silence is the worst criticism."

"As it turned out, she was planning our downfall. Company money turned up missing. Evidence was planted that implicated me. I went to jail on our wedding day. It was all Sylvia's doing. She knew the cops who arrested me, somehow got them to deny me a phone call until Monday. Meanwhile, she broke into our apartment and cleaned out my stuff to make it look like I'd left you for good."

"And she stole your money?"

"I believe so."

"How?"

"Only way I can figure, she'd forged my name on some paperwork."

"Why didn't you report her, turn her in, and prove she forged the papers?"

"The actual documents disappeared from the

bank's records. She must've had someone on the inside."

"Who *is* this woman?"

"She has her claws in a lot of powerful people, friends in high places, gets what she wants every time. High maintenance, demanding, uses her body like a checkbook. You were a breath of fresh air in my life, and she ruined it for us. By the time I got my freedom back, you were gone, and I knew if I went after her, she'd come up with some other scheme to get me thrown back in jail, or worse."

"Worse?" She leaned forward. "You mean she might have killed you?"

"I don't know, but I wasn't taking any chances. You had safely gone off the radar, I hoped, and I made a beeline for the recruiter's office. I had to get lost too."

"And now here we are, together again."

"What are the odds? You and me in the same city a half a world away from San Diego? Do you believe in destiny?"

"I believe in love."

"I love you, Marianne. That's never changed throughout this entire ordeal."

She sighed. "I can't say the same because I didn't know the facts. I hated you with every fiber of my body."

He leaned forward and gathered her hands in his. "That's what Sylvia wanted."

"Well, she failed, Jake."

"She did? How?"

"Because I do still love you. I want us to work now more than ever."

He clenched his jaw so he wouldn't shout with glee. Instead, he turned to the bad news. "It's not over yet."

Her fingers clutched his fingers. "Why? What do you mean?"

"She's here...I mean there. In Berlin."

"She found you?"

"And she knows you're here. She has pictures."

Marianne's eyes widened. "That guy on the rooftop."

"She's not working alone."

"What does she want?"

"Me."

"You?"

"She has this crazy notion that I'm going to marry her. Forget about everything that's happened. Put things back the way they were before I met you."

"And if you don't?"

He didn't know how to tell her, or even if he should tell her, that Sylvia had made an off-the-wall threat against her, but Marianne had the right to know. "I'm not saying for sure that you're in danger, but just in case, watch your back."

Panic welled in her eyes. "She'll come after me...to do what? Talk to me? Threaten me? Kill me?"

"Not while I'm alive."

"Jake, oh my God." She shot out of her chair, dropped into his lap, and looped her arms around his neck. "We're going to stop her, once and for all. You and I."

"How? She's like a bad dream, keeps coming back."

"Then we have to put her away for a long time."

"That won't be easy. She covers her tracks. And she has friends in high places."

"She must have a weakness, and we're going to find it. For us. For our future."

To hear her talk like this, using the words *us* and *we* to describe the future, for that he'd fight a million Sylvias, though he had no idea how. "I'm in. Let's go get her."

She planted a kiss on his lips, warm, wanting, and breathy, her arms locked around him, her fingers combing through his hair. The best kiss ever—

"Hummph." The waiter cleared his throat. "Your desserts, if you please."

She kept kissing him. He kept kissing her. Tongues tasting tongues. Her fragrance filling him with desire. He had won her back, finally, the Marianne he'd known and loved for so long.

She broke away, like the sun leaving the sky. "Guess we better have dessert," she whispered in his ear, then gave his earlobe a little nip.

Everyone in the café was watching them. As she reseated herself, the waiter set the desserts on the table, and the other patrons started clapping.

"Love is splendid," he said and backed away.

Jake smiled and nodded to the crowd. This night, this time, this place, this was the happiest he'd been in years.

"Dig in," Marianne said, armed with a giant spoon.

The desserts were truly elegant. The waiter had delivered Marianne's chocolate mousse on a white plate adorned with fresh strawberry, kiwi, and orange slices, sprinkled with a dusting of powdered sugar. Jake's dessert was simple yet divine, a vanilla pudding served in a flute with tangerine slices decorating the rim of the glass.

After dessert and coffee, Jake helped her don her shawl then placed his arm around her shoulder and escorted her outside. Walking through the town, she gazed up at thousands of stars that sparkled like diamonds above them. The moon, just peeping over the horizon, glowed white and proud.

"That's the biggest moon I've ever seen," she said, breathless.

Jake held her tight while looking at the heavenly sight. He didn't know which was more beautiful, Marianne or the moon.

"Where are we going now?" she asked, moonlight glinting from her upturned eyes.

"The *Kaiserhaus*. It's like a castle. And tonight it's Marianne's castle."

"Are you my knight in shining armor?"

"If you will be my damsel in distress."

"Oh, Sir Jake, save me." She giggled.

Continuing their stroll toward the *Kaiserhaus*, he had to be careful not to take a misstep on the uneven cobblestone pathway. Not much worse than a knight in shining armor landing flat on his face, which reminded him of the history that played out on this very ground beneath them. "Under this path lies a stone foundation, all that's left of the Church of Our Lady, which stood for five hundred years before it finally collapsed into ruin in 1722."

"It was gone before America was born."

"But its stones were salvaged for the construction of this..." He led her to a rise. Beyond stood the *Kaiserhaus*, its windowed walls and steep gables ablaze in the yellow glow of floodlights.

She gasped and placed her hand on her heart. "It's beautiful."

"Marianne..." He couldn't resist the temptation any further and abruptly took her into his arms. Without waiting for a reaction, he pressed a tender kiss on her forehead, and then trailed his mouth slowly down her cheek to her moist lips. He felt her body yield to his embrace as her eyes closed and her lips parted. She seemed to melt into him, as if every fiber of her body relinquished control to his loving touch. He wanted to gently lay her down on the courtyard grass and make love in the shadow of the *Kaiserhaus*. That would be a memory—

She stiffened as if suddenly aware of his thoughts.

He stopped kissing her, but held her close and inhaled her perfumed scent. "I want you, Marianne."

"Jake, no."

He exhaled a ragged breath and whispered, "We'll take it slow. Don't worry."

"No doesn't mean go slow, Jake. It means stop.

We're not going to do anything out here."

"I know we're not," he breathed. "It's just that you make me crazy."

"The feeling's mutual. Trust me."

He hugged her tight against him and concentrated on reining in his raging emotions.

"Can we go in my castle?"

Releasing her from his embrace, he took her by the hand, "Come with me," and led her up stone steps inside the bastion to the top level's arched windows. This would be a perfect vantage point to view the evening lights. Although Goslar was a small town of 46,000 citizens, the carpet of twinkling lights below seemed to mirror the reflection of the stars above.

Turning around and resting his back against the worn brick wall, he marveled at the scene. Everything seemed so unreal, yet here he was with Marianne. He felt as if their lives were supposed to be like this forever. She cuddled against his shoulder and slipped her arm around his side. He felt warm as she snuggled in closer.

"This is special, Marianne."

"Jake?"

"Yes?"

"Take me back to our room."

***

Marianne almost dragged Jake up the narrow stairs to their room. He appeared to have a hard time unlocking the door due to her nibbling on his earlobe.

"Hurry up," she whispered. "I want you. I want you now."

"Hold on to your panties, will ya?" He managed to get the door open.

They tumbled into the room while groping at each other's clothes and kicking off their shoes. While he untucked her blouse, she worked on a stubborn button on his shirt. "It's stuck."

"Rip it."

She laughed and tore off the button, pulling his shirt wide open to take a good look. Streetlight through the window illuminated his broad chest and tight abs. As she reached out to touch his solid pecks, her blouse suddenly slid up, pushed her arms upward, and blocked her view of him as he yanked the blouse over her head.

Even before her hair tumbled back to her shoulders, his lips met hers with passionate pressure, tender but firm, demanding her to respond with equal desire, tongues touching, quick breaths escaping in luscious pants while she went to work on his belt buckle. Pulling. Tugging.

The belt came loose. Button undone. Zipper down, leaving her amazed at how well she remembered her way into Jake's clothing.

His fingers plied the clips of her bra, and with the ease of a magician's trick, the tension released. He pulled down the shoulder straps and set her breasts free. His lips slipped from her mouth to her chin to her throat to her chest, leaving a trail of fiery hot kisses.

"Oh, yes, Jake." She thrust her breasts forward to meet his advance. His lips surrounded her left nipple, and his tongue flicked the erect and throbbing flesh. Sparks flew through her chest and down into her belly, scattering butterflies along the way.

She yanked his open shirt off his shoulders, let it fall to the floor while his eager fingers found the waist button of her skirt. Within a second, she was stepping out of it, turning Jake toward the bed, and shoving him backward. He let go of her nipple as he fell.

The bedsprings groaned under his weight.

He looked amazing. So strong. So male. Pants wide open, bare chest, powerful arms reaching for her. Instead of accepting his invitation, she grabbed his pant legs and pulled off his jeans. She could see the bulge in his underwear and remembered the times before the disastrous wedding when she couldn't get enough of what he had to offer. Morning, noon, night, it made no difference. Bedrooms, hotel rooms, staircases, elevators, closets, the places didn't matter either. God how she loved this man, and heaven had somehow favored that love and brought it back to her in Berlin.

She dropped her panties and stood naked before him, her heart beating like the flutter of angel wings.

"Marianne," he breathed. "You are amazing." His smoky eyes made her feel as if he thought he was looking at a goddess.

"You haven't seen anything yet." She flung herself on top of him. His musky-sweet scent inflamed her desire from head to toe.

He hugged her close, her breasts pressed hard against his chest, and she felt his complete arousal against her thigh. All that mattered tonight was her and Jake. The love they had for each other was newly rekindled and now billowing into a wild fire. All enveloping. All giving. All taking. All consuming. He would be hers. She would be his. There was no stopping them now.

She slid her hand under his elastic waistband and touched him.

He drew in a breath.

She covered his mouth with hers and slipped her hand down deeper, her fingers exploring territory they had not explored in years. Her core throbbed with need. His arousal felt hot against her palm, like it would burst into flame at any moment. She squeezed him. His tongue pushed into her mouth. She felt a gush of warmth between her legs. There was no doubt. She wanted him as much as he wanted her.

She drew back and gazed down at him, his face aglow in the dim light, his eyes shiny around the edges as if rimmed with tears of joy. "I love you, Jake."

"You'll never regret it, ever again, Marianne."

"It feels good not to hate you anymore."

He raised his hips off the bed, a clear signal to remove his underwear and begin whatever was to come next.

Chapter SEVENTEEN

What Can I Write About Marianne?

She whose foot-fall makes heads to turn and eyes to glaze.

She whose smile melts the morning frost and heats the imagination.

She whose eyes, deep and full of mystery, causes me to take flight of fantasy and pure delight...

What Can I Write About Marianne?

This much is true.

This bit of earth resounds with the magnificence of Marianne.

How could she really be captured in words on a lowly piece of paper?

My task would never be complete, for there are not enough words, there is not enough time.

For I am intoxicated and awed by she whose heart will be forever mine.

EVERYTHING IN THE WORLD seemed to be going Marianne's way as she rode the bus through the noisy streets of Berlin. Jake's recent love letter rolled over and over in her mind, causing her to drift away in wild imaginings and feel a rush of warmth in her core as she recalled their most recent romantic escapade. A week had passed since then. Jake had been busy on diplomatic missions with the Major, but he was due back this evening.

Golden rays of sunlight danced through backlit orange leaves, announcing that autumn was in full swing. Since the weather had been exceptionally warm and beautiful this past summer, the upcoming winter wasn't expected to be fierce. She had visions of her and Jake enjoying weekend ski trips to the nearby Hartz Mountains.

Prichard Strasse. This is the street I want.

She reached up and pulled the rope to let the driver know she wanted to get off at the next stop. As the bus pulled up to the curb, its tires made a crunching sound on fallen dry leaves.

She hopped out. The afternoon air felt crisp and clean, and she breathed it in as she carried two grocery bags heavy with ingredients for their evening dinner. She trudged up the steps to Jake's apartment.

Balancing the bags between her hip and the door, she rummaged through her shoulder bag and located the spare key Jake had given her. This was the first time she'd come to his place, and she wished he could have been with her, even carry her across the threshold. That would have been very romantic. She slid the key into the lock, turned it two revolutions, as he'd instructed, and shoved open the door.

Once inside, she glanced around the room.

Big place.

She expected to see his apartment strewn with papers and dirty laundry based on the fact that he was a bachelor. But by the sight of this sparkling clean room, it was apparent that he didn't fit the mold. She immediately located the kitchen and started toward it, noting a small wall clock that displayed *1:00.*

She had plenty of time to fix dinner.

After placing both bags on a counter by the stove, she began to organize her cooking plans. As she reached inside one of the bags, her ears picked up a strange sound. She froze as she cocked her head to listen. It sounded as if water was running.

How strange. It must be the neighbor's loud plumbing.

She chalked it up to thin walls and resumed her task. A few moments later, she heard another noise, but this time it wasn't running water. A door had creaked open.

Now that sound didn't come from the neighbor's door.

Floorboards creaked. Like it or not, she had company.

She snatched up a frying pan and spun around to face a potential assailant but dropped her jaw in astonishment at the sight of a raven-haired woman clad only in a white towel, standing in the kitchen doorway.

"Who are you?" Marianne's voice betrayed her sudden shock. She began to feel sick with fright.

Leaning against the doorframe, the woman took a drag from her cigarette, eyed Marianne from her ankles to the top of her head, and gave her a haughty appraisal.

She reared back with the frying pan. "What are you doing here?"

The strangely familiar woman adjusted her towel over her breasts then tipped her head back and exhaled a long stream of smoke. "I should be the one asking the questions. Who are *you*?"

Marianne swung the pan as a warning. "Get out."

The woman reached for the wall phone, not a foot from her and lifted the receiver. "Fine, I'll just call the police."

"I'm Jake's girlfriend. You'd better leave."

She snorted. "Girlfriend? Really?"

"You have no right to be here."

"Wanta bet?" The woman slammed down the receiver so hard it bounced off the hook and hung by the cord. "I'm Jake's wife."

"The hell you are. He's not married."

"We got married in Las Vegas a few years ago, and I finally found him in Berlin."

Marianne tried to wrap her brain around that. Jake had said he was single when they met. Had he lied about that?

The woman adjusted her towel once more, and with a polished nail, tapped her cigarette. Ashes showered onto the floor. Twisting her mouth into a wicked smile, she added, "Jake's always been a little kinky." She winked and licked her lips. "Are you here for this evening's sex party? I hope we can be a happy threesome."

Marianne was speechless. What was going on? Who was this awful woman? Why was she here? Her mind whirled in a funnel of chaos. She wanted to run, but her legs were suddenly made of stone. "He's not having a sex party tonight, at least not with the likes of you."

The woman frowned. "Honey, don't be sad. Jake's not boyfriend material. He likes to fool around too much, but if you are into that scene, I'm certainly game." She sauntered toward her and began to open the towel.

Marianne felt her face flush. Her throat grew parched, and a full-blown panic attack set in. "Don't come near me. I swear. I'll clobber you."

The woman dropped her towel, exposing every inch of her nakedness. "Come on. We could have some fun before Jake gets here."

Marianne stumbled backward and collided with the counter. Only one doorway. One way out. She'd have to get past Jake's phantom wife. But the woman was crazy. And she wasn't the least bit afraid of a frying pan. "You'd better stop before I hurt you."

She stopped. "What's the matter, honey?" Her tongue licked her upper lip as she cupped her breasts in her upturned palms. "Don't you want what you see?"

Her fight-or-flight response switched to flight. "Let me get out of here. That's all I want."

"You'll have to leave the frying pan. I'm sure it's not yours."

Marianne dropped the pan; it clanged on the floor, and held her hands out in surrender. "I don't want any trouble."

"Jake will be so disappointed that he lost

tonight's threesome partner."

Scooting around the naked woman, Marianne wanted to scream, but she couldn't; her throat had tightened that much. The room spun, and she feared that she'd vomit being this close to such a disgusting woman.

"Bye now," she sang.

Marianne jumped over the dropped towel and dashed out the kitchen doorway. She ran to the front door. The woman's laughter followed her all the way to her car. She jumped in and slammed the door. Catching her breath, the shock of this lewd encounter waned, and she wondered if she'd just come face-to-face with Sylvia.

Then the strangest feeling came over her. Sent goose bumps up the back of her neck and made her hair roots tingle. She had seen that face before.

***

Jake bounded up the steps, two at a time, to his apartment door, careful not to muss the bouquet of flowers he carried. After a three-country, multi-meeting trip with the Major, he was eager to see Marianne.

After he opened the front door, he noticed the bedroom door was slightly ajar. He always left it wide open. Perhaps she was taking a nap, or better yet, maybe she had a nice surprise in store for him. It was easy to imagine her wearing a sexy negligee and lying in wait on the bed.

He placed the bundle of yellow and white daisies

into a vase, then arranged it as the centerpiece on the dining room table. Then tip-toeing to the bedroom, he hoped to catch Marianne asleep...or better yet... As he approached the slightly opened door, he stopped short at the sight of a shapely leg visible beyond the gap. And brightly painted toenails. A towel above the bent knee.

Wow.

He pushed open the door.

The towel dropped to the floor.

For a split second, Jake thought he was dreaming, and then the dream turned into a nightmare as the initial shock of seeing Sylvia dumped his brain down a dark hole. His heart about stopped, and he feared for Marianne's safety. "Where is she?"

"Who, darling?"

"Marianne."

"She stopped by earlier but left when she realized you already had company for this evening."

Anger damn near blinded him. "What did you tell her, you bitch?"

"I tried to be sociable," Sylvia mewed. "But she's not very friendly."

"Get out of my house."

She settled on his bed and arched her back, showing off the perkiness of her erect nipples. "Come on now, Jake. It's your turn to be sociable."

"What are you trying to prove?"

Sylvia chuckled as she tipped back her head and shook her long black hair. "You should have seen her face when I told her that we were married."

"Married," Jake shouted. He felt light-headed.

How can this be happening?

"I love Marianne. You're not going to ruin it for us this time."

Sylvia sat up. Her eyebrows formed an evil V. "Is that right?"

He didn't like her challenging tone but matched it with his own. "Get out before I call the police."

She leaped from the bed with feline grace. "Before you do that..." She stormed to the dresser and lifted a photo she must've placed there earlier. "Have a look at this."

He scowled. "What kind of bullshit have you come up with this time?" But one look at the photo knocked the air from his lungs. Not the blurry subject of the photo, a woman posing, but the couple in the background, sitting at a small table, Marianne kissing another man. It had to be Heinrich. But they were just friends.

"There has to be a logical explanation," he mumbled.

"Don't waste your time on her. She already has another lover. She's been sleeping with him all this time."

"You don't know that for sure."

She grinned a wicked grin. "You want to see the other pictures?"

"You're bluffing."

"Try me."

He really didn't want to see them. Besides,

whatever she and Heinrich had, that was in the past, before Goslar, before they gave their hearts to each other, before they decided to fight back together. Sylvia's divide-and-conquer strategy might have almost worked, but this time love would conquer all.

He glared at Sylvia. "Doesn't matter anymore." He tossed the picture on the bed. "I want my money."

Lazing back down on the bed and settling into a suggestive pose, Sylvia purred, "Be a good boy and you just might earn it back." She patted the bedcover. "Care to start right now?" She spread her legs as if that would seal the deal.

Jake swallowed his disgust for this skank. There was no way he was going to fall into her trap, no matter how hard she tried to seduce him. He scooped her off the bed and carried her out of the bedroom.

She squirmed and giggled as if she thought this was an act of endearment. "Jake…don't. Not in the living room."

He opened the front door with one hand and dumped her onto the concrete outside. "Go to hell, Sylvia." He slammed the door.

"Jake," she screamed. "You can't do this to me. I love you."

Jake had to laugh. The more of a scene she made, the more attention she would draw to herself, and the more likely the police would respond and arrest her for indecent exposure. He peeked out the front room curtain in time to see her get to her feet and hide her breasts behind folded arms. She was a beauty to behold, but beneath that beautiful skin, she was an ugly, two-headed monster.

A lifetime ago, he thought he loved her in spite of her pushy attitude and demand for attention. She could have been the poster girl for high maintenance. Thankfully, Marianne came along and saved him from a lifetime of putting up with her bullshit, or a divorce that would have cost him everything. Hell, he'd lost everything to her anyway.

She stormed down the steps toward the parking lot and sprinted to a little red Yugo. As he watched her scramble into the front seat, he hoped she had a spare key.

Chapter EIGHTEEN

MARRIED?

Marianne flung herself on top of her bed. That had to have been the lie of the century, and that woman must've been Sylvia. Jake had said she was a real bitch, but from what Marianne had seen, Sylvia went beyond bitch, beyond slut, beyond whore to something evil only the devil could love. How could Jake have ever gotten caught up in that woman's claws?

She decided to call him to tell him what had happened, though it was all too crazy to be believable. Never before had a woman propositioned her, especially a naked woman. She rolled over to the bedside phone and held her breath as she dialed his apartment, but all she heard was a busy signal. It wasn't hard to picture the phone off the hook while Sylvia had her way with him.

He must've been surprised to see her there when he got home from work. Maybe even angry. Definitely, he wasn't planning on a threesome for tonight. He had expected a home-cooked dinner. So Sylvia was lying when she'd said she and Jake had planned a sex party. The question was, how did Sylvia know about their dinner plans? And how did she get in?

Oh, but Sylvia was capable of breaking and entering. She'd gotten into their last apartment and moved out Jake's belongings. No forced entry, yes, she was a pro.

But where had she seen Sylvia before? Downtown? On the subway? Faces came to mind, flashes of recollection, mostly blurry, but none bore Sylvia's likeness. How about at work? The American Consulate. The Passport office. And then she remembered the black-haired bitch who had lost her passport. What was her last name? Where was she staying?

Marianne sat straight up on the bed. She had to get to the office.

**

The image of Sylvia oozed like a nasty oil spill in the back of Marianne's mind, reigniting her anger and distain as she signed in with security at the American Consulate. Would she ever get the memory of the naked woman's breasts out of her head? Some serious psychotherapy was in order.

But was she ever married to Jake? Maybe he'd fudged on that detail, saying Sylvia was an old girlfriend instead of his wife. She should kick herself for even thinking it was possible. Still, the truth was in here somewhere. She unlocked her office and turned on the light.

Sitting at her computer, she turned on the monitor. Green letters on a black background asked her to sign in with her password. She typed

Jake$is%an#idiot and got into her database. One day she would have to change her password.

"Hmmmm...come on, already...where is she...where is she?"

Having forgotten the rude woman's last name, she'd searched the keyword *Sylvia*. Hundreds of records scrolled by, flashing names and pictures and stopping only on those that matched the keyword. A blonde from Detroit. Lots of brunettes. Too young. Too old. Too ugly, then bingo. She could never forget that face.

Sylvia Maderas.

"Not Sylvia Adams," she muttered.

She scanned the data file. According to the information she'd supplied on her passport form, she was single. She'd said she and Jake got married a few years ago. So either she lied on her passport application or she lied about ever being married to Jake. The first possibility would get her thrown in jail for perjury. She wouldn't have done that, in fact, she would have bragged about being married to Jake.

Then Marianne remembered how adamant the woman was about not being married.

Yes, Sylvia Maderas was lying. Jake had told her the truth.

A twinge of guilt niggled at Marianne for even thinking Jake would have lied to her. As she stared at Sylvia's passport photo, a nasty taste formed in Marianne's mouth. "You're not taking him away from me this time, bitch."

***

The next morning, the passport office was jammed with people. The entire staff was scurrying as fast as they could to keep the lines moving. Marianne took a few moments of refuge in her office to give Jake a call. She hadn't slept well last night, and she had to know what happened when Jake got home. He picked up on the first ring.

"Hello."

"So that was Sylvia Maderas."

"I'm sorry she showed up like that," he said. "Really sorry."

"I tried to call you but all I got was a busy signal."

"The stupid phone was off the hook."

She remembered the receiver bouncing off the hook and hanging by the cord. No wonder—

"After I discovered that, I tried calling you but you didn't answer."

Of course, she'd left for the office right away.

"I should have seen this coming." His voice was filled with irritation. "Did she hurt you?"

"No, but she is pretty scary. Beautiful but scary. Did she stay long?"

"She tried to seduce me."

"Me too."

"I had to throw her out. Naked, in fact." He laughed. "She sat in her car for an hour, 'til I brought her purse out to her. But I wouldn't give her back her clothes. If she wasn't mad before, she certainly is now."

"She told me that you two were married a few

years ago."

"We can't stop her from dreaming, but we can sure as hell wake her ass up."

"I recognized her from the passport office. We'd made her a replacement passport shortly after I started work here."

"Damn. So she knows who you are and where to find you."

Marianne felt a pang of dread in her chest. "You think she'll come after me?"

"Don't put anything past her. She's desperate."

Marianne almost relished the idea of a cat fight with Sylvia. Almost. "Can I see you today?"

"The major needs me to go on another trip with him. The Berlin Wall discussions are gaining traction, and I have to be there. Will you be all right?"

"Depends on how desperate she is."

"Watch your back, Marianne."

"You be careful, too."

She hung up and stared at the phone. When Jake returns from his trip, they'd have to pay Sylvia a visit, take the battle to the enemy, head-on.

Chapter NINETEEN

MARIANNE SAT IN THE passenger seat of Jake's Porsche and double-checked the address on her note pad. "This is the address Sylvia gave me. Her passport was delivered here."

"Let's hope that missing paperwork from the bank is here too."

"I would have destroyed it, but she's so narcissistic, I'm betting she would have kept it for a souvenir to remind her how cunningly she'd ripped you off."

Jake parked around the corner from the boarding house but close enough in case they had to make a run for it. "Never thought I'd be the one breaking and entering her place." He laughed, but his tone carried a nervous edge. "I don't see a red Yugo around here, so if we're lucky, she'll be gone for a while."

Marianne got out of the car. "Then let's not waste any time."

The boarding house front door was unlocked, as most any hostel or hotel's would be, as each individual room was locked. She followed Jake up the stairs, looking around for any watchful eyes. Stalking down the hall, she caught her breath as she found the room number they were looking for. "Here. Room

324."

"I'm surprised it's not room 666," Jake muttered.

"How do we get in?"

"Easy." He pulled a credit card from his wallet and jimmied the lock. It opened easily.

"Where did you learn to do that?"

"Doug Hanson, you remember him?"

"Yes, your lieutenant friend at the Officer's Ball."

"He thinks Sylvia used a credit card to gain access to our apartment without a key. To prove his point, he showed me how to do it. Won't work on a dead bolt, but doorknob locks are fair game, especially in these old buildings."

Inside, she determined there were only two rooms, the front room and a back bedroom. The entire place was dark and reeked of cigarette smoke. Jake found a light switch, flipped it on, and made a beeline for the bedroom. As Marianne followed, she gasped in fright at the motion of a woman... "Oh, my gosh!"

Jake ran out of the bedroom. "What is it?"

"I passed this mirror and I freaked when I saw my reflection. I thought it was Sylvia."

"Sheesh! Don't scare me like that." He rubbed his forehead. "How about standing guard at the window? Keep an eye out for that red Yugo." He stalked back to the bedroom.

Marianne rushed to the closed drapes and pushed them slightly open. A wedge of sunlight angled across the floor. The room overlooked the street and a small parking lot. No red Yugo anywhere to be seen.

Jake rummaged through Sylvia's belongings. "Nothing here," he said. "Some clothes in the closet and dresser drawers, sex toys in the nightstand, and that's about it. I don't see anywhere she might have stashed those missing papers." Jake's voice sounded discouraged. He returned to the front room, scouted the bookcase and end-tables. "Nothing. She must've gotten rid of them or left them in San Diego."

Marianne didn't think so. Not Sylvia. Those papers were dear to her. She'd keep them close to her heart. Somewhere...she'd flown in to Berlin, maybe an airport locker. "Look for a key, Jake."

"I didn't see one. It's no use."

"Hmmm," she murmured as a thought bubbled up. If Sylvia had flown in, then where was her luggage? "Did you see any suitcases?"

"No, I didn't."

"She has to have at least one suitcase around here, stashed somewhere big enough..."

They both eyed the bed at the same time. Jake dropped to his knees and lifted the bed skirt. "Voilà! Two of them." He pulled out the first one.

Marianne opened it. The stink of old sweat hit her like a club. "Phwew! This woman needs to do some serious laundry." She held her head to the side, keeping her eyes on the suitcase while she rifled through Sylvia's dirty clothes. "No papers here."

Jake had already pulled out the second suitcase and opened it. "Well, lookie here." In among some personal items lay two manila envelopes.

Marianne slammed her suitcase closed and

pushed it back underneath the bed. "Let's have a look."

The envelopes weren't sealed, so it was easy for Jake to open them. As he sorted through the documents, he said, "Wow," and beamed at her. "The missing bank papers, all right, a forged power of attorney and a list of investment accounts where the money was transferred." He studied the numbers. "But there's more money here than I had in my bank accounts. Oh my God." He looked up. "It's the money she embezzled from the company, as well."

"What's in the other envelope?"

"Let's see." He opened the envelope and pulled out a bunch of papers. "It's a report of some kind. From a private investigator." Jake groaned. "This is how she found me." He held up an accompanying business card. "And here's the guy who did her dirty work."

"It's all the proof you need to clear your name. Let's get out of here."

"It's not that easy," he said, holding his ground. "If she finds out these papers are missing, she'll flee the country before I get my money back. We need to make copies and return the originals."

Marianne didn't like that idea. "That means we'll have to come back here."

"It's the only way to be sure she's not spooked. Who knows how long it'll take to convince the cops to act on this information?"

She thought of the copy machine in her office. "We'll have to hurry."

Jake high-fived her, and then pushed the suitcase under the bed.

**

The copier chugged as it slowly churned out copies of Sylvia's *souvenirs*. Marianne sorted them in the exact order they were in originally.

"Can this thing go any faster?" Jake looked as jumpy as a cricket on a hot skillet.

"Almost done. See if you can find some coffee. It'll give you something to do."

Jake went off in search of coffee, and by the time he returned with a cup for her, she was stuffing the originals back into the envelopes. "This was the easy part. Now we have to put these back without being caught."

He set his coffee on the copy machine. She drank hers on the way back to the boarding house.

Jake looked nervous, a little pale and sweaty, as he parked the car around the corner in the same spot as before. Marianne put on a brave face. "We can do this, Jake." She crumpled her empty cup. "We can put her away for good."

Jake gave her a reassured smile and hopped out of the car. "Talk about good luck. I don't see any red Yugos."

Marianne joined him, envelopes in hand. "You know what they say about good luck? It can only turn bad."

"I'm trying to be optimistic here."

They slinked up the stairs, opened the door with

the credit card key, and breathed a sigh of relief that they'd gotten in without being spotted. She handed him the envelopes. "Make it fast."

Jake dashed into the bedroom to re-stash the documents in the suitcase.

Just then, she heard the sound of laughter coming from down the hall. She'd heard that laughter before. Sylvia.

Marianne sprinted to the window and looked out. Sure as hell, a red Yugo was parked down there. "Shit! She's here, Jake." She felt her face go pallid. The blood drain from her head made her dizzy. Her heart jammed against her ribs like a caged squirrel. She looked for another exit, but there was only the window and the one door.

A key clicked into the lock.

"Get in here," Jake hissed.

She made the bedroom just as the door opened, letting in Sylvia's loud laughter.

"Jake? Where are you," she whispered.

"Under here," he whispered back.

She dove for the floor and crawled under the bed, chased by Sylvia's voice.

"You're so lean and muscular." Her words slurred drunkenly.

A man's voice, "Lady, you've got to be the hottest number this side of the Berlin Wall."

Boisterous laughter.

Jake glanced at Marianne, put his fingers to his lips in a shushing gesture. He still held the envelopes, not having had enough time to stash them. She didn't dare say a word.

Sylvia giggled. "Step into my parlor said the spider to the fly."

"You don't have to ask me twice," the man replied.

Crap, they're coming in here.

Wait it out; that was all they could do. And pray neither coughed or sneezed or swallowed.

A pair of high heels approached the bed, followed by dark leather shoes. One pair went one way, one the other, leaving bare feet, Sylvia's, and socks, the man's. A dress hit the floor. Then trousers. Then panties and bra, then boxers. The drawn curtains left it dark enough in the room that anything else would have been hard to see.

The bed creaked as Sylvia plopped down, the mattress sagging to nearly an inch of Marianne's backside.

"Come to Mamma," Sylvia's voice purred.

Within a moment, the man was barefoot and jumped aboard. The bed sank deeper, the springs just barely touching Marianne. She tried to make herself skinnier, but as the man rolled on top of Sylvia, Marianne had to exhale and scoot closer to the edge. Jake had done the same on the other side of the bed. If Sylvia and her man friend got to jumping and humping up there, Marianne feared she and Jake would be pummeled to death.

"Not so fast, *mein heir*." Sylvia's laugh wielded a wicked edge. "You've been a very bad boy and must be punished."

Jake turned to Marianne and grinned. She rolled her eyes and mouthed the words, *just great*. A little S&M for the afternoon's delight. Why not?

Sylvia hopped off the bed. Her feet crossed the room, and then returned. The bed creaked again as she straddled her lover. "Give me your wrist."

A pair of handcuffs clicked. The bed springs shifted. Another click.

Marianne imagined the scene playing out only a foot above her, the naked man splayed out as a sacrifice for the whore demon, Sylvia.

Then the party began.

"Hang on for the ride, buster."

The mattress bounced up and down as Sylvia went to work on her lover. The creaking of the bed competed with her squeals of lustful delight. "Ooo, ooo oh, yeah." The man was moaning and honking like a donkey. "Honk, honk, hee haw." No uglier a love scene could Marianne have ever imagined possible. Or noisier. The words *nympho from hell* flashed through her mind. She squeezed her eyes tight and wished for the orgy to subside.

"Ooo, ooo oh, yeah."

"Ride it, baby, ride it. Honk, honk, hee haw."

A shuffling sound next to her popped her eyes open. Jake had crawled out from under the bed. She wanted to scream *what the hell are you doing* but caught herself. The bed frame's banging and the springs' squeaking masked the sound of the suitcase sliding out. She could see him keep low as he opened it, inserted the envelopes, and closed the lid.

"Do it, baby, do it. I'm ready. I'm ready."

"Don't you dare finish. Ooo, ooo oh, yeah."

Springs squeaked like the violin strings of Hades. Jake slid the suitcase back into place.

"Keep it up," Sylvia screamed. "Keep it up. I'm almost there."

"Honk, honk, hee haw."

Marianne wished she hadn't drunk that coffee. Her stomach was about to expel it. And when she saw Jake crawling around the bed on his hands and knees, her throat seized around her windpipe. What was he doing?

"I'm there. I'm there," Sylvia screamed in orgasmic relief. "Oh yes. Oh yes. Don't stop."

The bed frame started hopping around under their violent throes of passion.

Jake waved her to come out.

"Honk, honk, hee haw."

She shook her head. Maybe they'd finish and leave soon.

Jake persisted in his waving motions, his brow furrowed with insistence.

"Yes! Yes! Yes!" Sylvia was a crazy woman on steroids, screaming and moaning like she was being whipped and poked at the same time.

Fear struck Marianne's heart with the idea of getting caught. How long would she and Jake spend in a German jail? But he was right. She had to move now, while the lovers were totally involved in their own sick worlds. It was all or nothing, now or never. She abandoned her safe haven.

Jake grabbed her hand, pulled her clear of the bed, and keeping low, she crawled with him out of the bedroom under a cloak of sexual madness.

In the front room, she got to her feet and tiptoed to the front door. Jake silently opened it, and then it was a mad dash down the stairs and out to his car.

She climbed into her seat, breathless, as Jake jumped in behind the wheel. She looked at him, the shock and awe on his face, and wondered if she sported the same expression.

Then he smiled. "We did it."

She couldn't help but laugh, but in a strange way, she was a little horny for him right now.

Chapter TWENTY

JAKE ENTERED CLAY HEADQUARTERS, the old grey building of 766MID, and met with intelligence agent Sam Clawson. He had called earlier and said his team of volunteer investigators had deciphered the papers from Sylvia's suitcase.

Sam led him to a guest conference area near the main lobby. Jake took a seat, anxious but hopeful. "What do you think?"

"Where the hell did you find this woman?" Sam set the papers on the table and remained standing.

Jake glanced at the familiar papers. "What's that got to do with anything?" He didn't mean to sound impatient, but he was at his wit's end with curiosity about how he could get his money back from Sylvia and clear his name.

"She's one clever crook."

"How did she do it?"

"She managed a complicated set of transfers from the company coffers to an offshore investment account in the Cayman Islands. The tricky part was the digital trail, which she wiped through a ghost account that she'd set up in your name. That's where the trail ended, and you were arrested."

"They dropped the charges with prejudice for lack of evidence."

"Only because they couldn't prove beyond a reasonable doubt that you owned that account, in fact, they couldn't prove anyone did. What these papers show and the prosecution didn't know is how she moved the money from there to accounts in her name." Sam's steel grey eyes stared off into the distance. It seemed as if he admired her cleverness.

"So you know where these accounts are now. That's great. Freeze them, subpoena them, and seize them, however you guys do it—"

"It's not that easy, Jake."

"Let's get the money, call the prosecutors. We've got her now."

"What the hell did you do to piss that lady off?"

"She's not a lady," Jake hissed.

Sam leaned over and tapped the papers with the tip of his pen. "This is the smoking gun you need to put her away for a long time."

Prison wouldn't suit Sylvia, not for one minute, but that was only half the battle. "How long will it take to get my money back?"

Sam crossed his arms and lowered his voice. "Sorry, Jake. The government, the courts, or even the World Bank can't touch the money in those offshore accounts."

The wind went out of his lungs. "There's got to be a way."

"Oh yes, there is a way. All you have to do is convince Sylvia to give it to you."

"She'll never do that, not in a million years."

"Then I hope you find solace in the fact that

she'll not be able to spend a nickel of it from behind bars. My people are working with the West Berlin authorities to issue an arrest warrant as we speak. They'll have her in custody within twenty-four hours."

"Wait, I mean, no. What's the rush? I need time to think. Once she's in jail, I'll never get my money."

"You're never going to get it anyway."

Visions of Sylvia behind bars screamed through his brain, no, not the visions, but Sylvia was doing the screaming. "Jail. Prison. Sam, that's the key, the leverage, the straw that'll break her back." Excitement tweaked his voice one pitch higher. "I've got an idea. But I'll need more time."

"I suppose I can hold off on the warrant. How long do you need?"

"I'll let you know." Jake rushed outside. He wanted to run down the sidewalk, leap in the air, and tap his heels together. But he didn't. Somehow, he had to warn Sylvia that the police were closing in on her.

***

The phone rang in a small, one-room flat situated in the French quarter of Berlin. On the forth ring, top notch investigator Damien Prue stepped out of the shower and answered the phone. "True Prue Investigations."

Dripping wet, he felt irritated that his shower had been cut short. However, phone calls typically meant money, and he needed every dime right now, especially since Sylvia Maderas stiffed him out of his latest fee.

"Damien Prue, please," a man's voice said.

"Who's asking?" Alarm bells rang in Damien's mind. This guy could be some woman's husband out to get his naughty pictures back.

"This is Jake Adams," the man said. "Do you remember that name? You did some work for Sylvia Maderas."

Damn. His target had found him out. Never before had this happened. The bitch probably gave him up. "How did you get my number?" he growled.

"It doesn't matter."

"Look." Damien threw a towel over his dripping hair. "It was just a job, nothing personal."

"I get it," Jake said. "I'm not calling about you investigating me."

"You're not pissed off?"

"I'm pissed off, all right. At Sylvia."

"Hey, I warned her to leave you alone. She repaid my good advice by not paying me for the job."

"I need your help."

Damien considered hanging up due to the strange circumstances of this call, but money was money. "I charge a hundred bucks an hour plus expenses."

"If I understand you right, she owes you some money."

"Yeah, a ton of money. A butt load of bucks. What about it?" Damien dried his underarms.

"You and I have a lot in common then."

Damien nodded. "So the bitch owes us both money. So what?"

"You want to get your money?"

"Cat got an ass?"

"I have an idea. Are you interested?"

"A hundred bucks an hour plus expenses."

"That's fine. This is what I need you to do."

Damien smiled for the first time in weeks.

***

Sylvia was brewing herself a cup of coffee when the phone rang. She wasn't supposed to have an espresso machine in her room, but the coffee in the community kitchen downstairs tasted like cat piss. "What is it?" she barked, hoping it wasn't management calling to throw a hissy about her breaking the house rules again.

"Madam, are you all right?" Damien's voice came over the line. He sounded concerned.

"What do you want, worm?"

"I need to tell you something."

"I thought I fired you."

"You did, but—"

"When I fire someone, they stay fired. And you're not getting any more money from me. You got that?" She slammed down the receiver. "Idiot."

The phone rang again. She picked up. "What the hell is the matter with you?"

"I call to give you a heads up, a warning, madam. I just overheard a most interesting conversation between the West Berlin Polizei and

American MPs."

That got her attention. "What did you hear?"

"They found your lost passport."

Adrenaline belted her bloodstream. "You mean the one *you* lost."

"It really doesn't matter, madam, they found your passport in the possession of an international drug smuggler named The Raccoon. He told the authorities that you gave it to him as collateral for a black tar heroin shipment that you're currently selling on the streets of West Berlin."

She felt as if she'd been punched in the gut. "That's not true," she screamed in the phone.

"It seems that madam has been very busy lately."

"A total lie!"

"Madam, I am not in a position to judge. I only called to warn you that the authorities are making plans to arrest you as we speak."

"Bullshit," she screamed louder, like Damien had a hearing problem, or if she screamed loud enough, the entire city would know she was innocent of any drug dealing. "I never did any of that."

"Madam, please don't scream at me. I am only the messenger."

"Why should I trust you? You're probably just yanking my chain because I didn't pay you."

"No, madam, I warn you because, if you are in jail, I will never get my money."

"You won't get your money anyway."

"A good deed is worth something, yes?"

"I don't believe you."

"That is up to you, madam, but if the police believe the Raccoon, what happens to you? You are arrested. It could take years to prove your innocence, but there is good news. West Berlin prisons aren't so bad compared to East Berlin prisons. They have much fewer rats and roaches."

"You should know."

"And those squirmy little bugs in the food, they are an acquired taste, but good protein."

"I'm not going to jail."

"Then you will be fine as long as you leave before the Polizei arrive."

She slammed down the phone again, not because she was annoyed with the weasel investigator, but because she had some serious packing to do.

***

Damien smiled with satisfaction. She had taken the bait. He knew Sylvia well enough to know that she would be scurrying out of town like a rat from a sinking ship. He'd parked his car up the street where he could watch the activity in front of the boarding house. Martin Savoy, his good friend and expert pocket picker sat next to him. Both had their eyes on the front door. Damien pictured Sylvia running around her room, stuffing things in her suitcases with reckless abandon.

"Are you sure she will leave town?" Martin asked him.

Damien glanced at him. "Prison for Sylvia would be like a nun in a whore house, or a whore in a nunnery, which ever you like."

Martin's mouth was missing a few teeth. Nothing a good dentist couldn't fix. Perhaps after this payment he would consider getting some new choppers.

"Is that her?" Martin pointed out.

Sylvia tromped down the stairs, lugging two suitcases, one in each hand, and a shoulder strapped purse. She opened the trunk of the red Yugo and tossed everything inside, then slammed the trunk closed.

"What'd I tell ya?" Damien said.

As the Yugo lurched off down the street, he started the engine of his Honda Accord and followed her, careful not to drive too close and arouse suspicion, yet not too far behind to lose her. He was used to tailing people, and he was very good at it. It was all about the chase.

Within a few minutes, she pulled into a bus terminal parking area. Damien stopped along the curb only a hundred feet away.

She lugged her suitcases inside.

"We better get into position," he told Martin. "See what bus she takes."

This was a plan-as-he-went assignment because he had no idea by which means Sylvia would leave West Berlin. He jumped from the car, joined Martin, and sprinted toward the terminal. To anyone around, they would only look like a couple of guys who were late to catch a bus.

Once inside the terminal, he spotted Sylvia

dragging her luggage away from the ticket window. He held Martin back and watched her trudge to a row of parked buses. She chose one with a marquee that read: *East Berlin Tours.*

The driver checked her ticket then tossed her suitcases into the luggage compartment. Clinging to her purse strap, she boarded the bus.

Damien and Martin rushed to the ticket booth and bought tickets to East Berlin, as well, and they too stepped onto the bus. Damien made sure he kept his face turned away from her as he walked down the aisle past her, then he and Martin took a seat a few rows behind her.

"Meinen Damen und Heren, does everyone have a passport?" the driver asked in German, and then in English. Everyone waved their passports in the air, including Damien and Martin, who paid particular attention to where Sylvia kept hers.

In Berlin, everyone carried proper papers, just in case of a random check, and those who did not, did so at their own peril.

Chapter TWENTY-ONE

FEELING ON EDGE, Sylvia opened her purse and withdrew her leopard-print wallet. The fine Italian leather felt cool in her hands, comforting her jittery nerves. Counting money was always a satisfying distraction. She was confident this bus would be the best way to get out of town in a hurry.

She thumbed through a wad of East German currency that she'd previously exchanged in case she had to flee West Berlin should Jake have turned her in to the authorities.

Always have an escape plan.

Even the temporary visa to enter East Berlin rested in the folds of her passport, which only moments ago she'd flashed to the bus driver and tucked back into her wallet.

The bus pulled out of the terminal. Sylvia nervously searched the streets for any sign of the West Berlin police who were coming to arrest her. She scrutinized passing cars for the word *Polizei* painted on the door. Thanks to the investigator's warning, it appeared she'd made her escape in the nick of time. She began to relax, let the tension in her shoulders loosen. Her breathing became calmer, and she wished she'd had time to finish her cup of espresso.

The respite didn't last long. The bus was approaching Checkpoint Charlie, the notorious border crossing between East and West Berlin. She held her breath in nervous anticipation of impending disaster. If the American guards knew of her warrant in West Berlin, they would not let her pass but arrest her on the spot.

Much to her surprise, the Americans waved the bus through the raised gate. It rumbled across no-man's land to the East Berlin checkpoint. The crossing gate was down, and the bus squealed to a stop.

A Russian guard stomped up the steps and onto the bus. As the driver displayed his passport, he and the guard traded a few remarks before the guard turned his eye toward the seated passengers. "Everyone have passports? Raise in air," he said in bad English and worse German.

Sylvia held up her passport as he tromped down the aisle, shooting quick glances at everyone's names. She didn't look at him but out the window as if enchanted by the goings on. He tromped back up front and mumbled something to the driver. They both laughed. All in a day's work for these guys. Mostly boring routine. After one final glance up the aisle, the guard patted the driver on the shoulder and exited the bus.

Sylvia realized she had been holding her breath and exhaled. It seemed like the worst was now over.

After the crossing gate rose, the bus lumbered through the checkpoint. Sylvia looked out the window, and for a fleeting moment, her eyes locked with the Russian guard's. Was it her imagination, or was he staring at her? Did he know who she was? Or perhaps his leer was just lustful interest.

As the bus maneuvered its way into East Berlin, she settled back in her seat, feeling more at ease. She reached into her purse and pulled out a compact and a lipstick tube. As she applied the bright red color to her lips, she pretended to study herself in the mirror while she considered the next part of her plan to switch buses to one bound for Geneva.

The bus stopped at a downtown shopping area for a one hour break. Sylvia slung her purse strap over her shoulder and got off. She felt somewhat safe at the moment. What better way to ease her tension than shopping? As she looked around, she found a jewelry store display window and marveled at the craftsmanship of East German jewelry. The diamonds looked to have been fine-cut, but a closer inspection was required before she would consider adding one of the more unique pieces to her collection. After all, she had money to burn in her offshore accounts.

Just as she turned for the doorway, the earth seemed to suddenly shift underneath her as she was shoved against the display window.

"Excuse me," a man's voice said from behind her.

She spun about to reprimand the clumsy lout who had crashed into her. "What's the matter with you? Are you drunk?"

"My pardon, madam," the young man stammered in broken English. "These sidewalks, they are uneven. Please to forgive me for tripping." He pointed to the poorly maintained cement then placed his palms together in a pleading gesture.

She hugged her purse close to her side, tossed her head in annoyance, and then waved him off. He might have been sexually interesting to her if he didn't have so many missing teeth.

The man scuttled away like a cockroach discovered in the light. She looked down at the sidewalk and stepped carefully as she started for the store entrance. The last thing she needed was to snap off one of her four-inch heels.

About to enter the store, she noticed a tour group enter a restaurant up the street. Having not eaten all day, she changed direction. The jewelry could wait for now. She checked over her shoulder for anyone following her, and then picked up speed to join the group.

Inside the restaurant, her eyes had to adjust to the low light. The sweet and robust aroma of food lifted her spirits. She was in a large room of wooden tables, and the décor was that of a hunting lodge. Thick beams traversed the ceiling where antler chandeliers glowed and flickered.

Based on the increasing level of laughter and conversation, everyone in the tour group seemed to be enjoying themselves. Almost every table was occupied. Harried wait staff scurried from table to table, jotting down orders and bumping into each other as they passed through double-doors to the kitchen.

Not feeling chatty, Sylvia searched the room for a table where she could sit by herself. Unfortunately, the seating was limited. She spied a vacant seat at a table where a young couple sat nuzzling each other's necks, obviously in love. "Great," she muttered, put on her happy face, and strolled over to the young couple's table. *"Guten Abend."* She motioned with her hand to the open chair.

The couple glanced up and smiled, and then the young man gestured for her to join them. The husband, Sylvia surmised by glancing down at his ring finger, attempted to speak to her in German but gave up when she shrugged as if she didn't understand a word he was saying. She felt relieved that her dinner companions would not be engaging her in any small talk.

Although the main dinner choices were limited: roast wild boar, chicken cordon bleu, or Jaeger Schnitzel, the wonderful rich smells emanating from the kitchen promised a hearty German meal. She ordered the schnitzel.

While she waited, she hailed a young sommelier and ordered an expensive bottle of merlot, which he promptly brought to the table along with a wine glass sporting a round, wide bowl. He poured a splash of wine into the glass and waited for her to taste it. The rich red wine warmed Sylvia's tongue, as well as the inside of her throat. *"Ja."* Sylvia nodded, indicating she wanted her glass filled and the bottle left on the table.

Everyone's dinners were served quickly due to

the tour bus's short stay, which suited Sylvia just fine. Her mouth watered at the sight of the breaded pork cutlet smothered with a rich sauce and sautéed mushrooms. She inhaled the heady aroma and cut into the meat. It was as tender as it looked, and she savored every bite.

Before long, the tour guide stood up and announced that everyone needed to wrap up their meals and pay their checks. The bus would be leaving shortly.

Satisfied, Sylvia decided that a good tip was in order for the excellent meal and service. She glanced to the wine bottle, hoping for one last splash of wine, but it was empty, having enjoyed it more than she realized.

The waiter presented her with the check and stood by awaiting payment.

A bit tipsy, she reached into her purse for her wallet but didn't feel it. Terror knifed her in the chest. It was here when she was on the bus. She reached into another pocket, furrowed her eyebrows, and shook her head in disbelief. Her wallet was gone.

How...when...what? She'd been robbed. A gnawing fear rose in her gut. She scrambled through her purse once more, hoping beyond hope she'd missed it somehow. "Damn."

The waiter scowled at her. "Is there a problem, madam?"

"My wallet, my money. Gone." And the worst part hit like a boxing glove blow to the head. Also gone were her passport and visa, which she had tucked into her wallet. Without them, she could never leave the country. She'd have to find an American Consulate to get a replacement passport. By now they would know about the arrest warrant. What the hell was she going to do? "Everything was stolen."

Any sympathy she hoped to gain seemed lost on the Germans. The waiter asked, "Must I call the manager?"

Fighting panic, she turned to the young couple. "Please, will you loan me the money?"

They shrugged as if they didn't understand a word she'd said.

Sylvia leaned to the folks seated at the table beside hers and asked if they would help her. They understood English and answered in English, "Sorry, but no."

She scanned the room, spotted the tour guide. Perhaps he could help her. "One moment," she said to the waiter, flew out of her chair, and rushed to him. "Please, my wallet has been stolen. I cannot pay my check. Please, will you cover me? I'll pay you back."

"Don't be absurd," the man said.

The manager joined them. "You must pay now or I will call the Polizei."

They would want to see her papers. She was screwed. Clutching her purse she realized who was to blame. That man who had run into her in front of the jewelry store. He was a pickpocket. She had to find him, and fast, but he was probably long gone.

"Damn," she muttered and took off for the door, barely escaping the meaty grasp of the restaurant

Stephanie Smith

manager's hand as he tried to stop her. She burst outside. Bright daylight blinded her. Her heels clacked on the uneven concrete as the manager's voice shouted out in German, "Stop her. Thief. Somebody stop her."

After three blocks, she ducked in an alley and leaned against a brick wall, hoping to catch her breath. "Double-damn." Her luggage was still on the bus. How would she ever get it back?

The sharp warble of a siren not far away jolted her back into a run. This was not what she had in mind for how her escape from West Berlin would go, but she vowed to find a way out of this mess.

She ran down the alley to another street, searching in vain for a crowd to get lost in. Her feet hurt from her high heels, so she leaned up against a lamppost and pulled off her shoes and tossed them into her purse. Just then, a white and green car turned the corner and drove slowly up the street in her direction. As the car neared, the word Polizei came into clear view.

"Crap." She didn't dare run and attract attention to herself, so she struck a sexy pose against the lamppost.

A blue light flashed on the car roof and accelerated toward her. Sylvia stood as still as a statue, willing herself to melt into the lamppost. She took notice of the two male occupants. They wore dark green shirts with white lettering on the sleeves: *Grenztruppen der DDR*, East German Border Guards.

Why would they be after me?

Her feet told her to run, but she held fast to the lamppost, her heart raging like a wild animal in a neck snare, until the police car sped past her and careened around the next corner.

Sylvia gulped a breath of fresh air. Not out of danger, she started walking down the street in the opposite direction, hoping to find a place crowded with people, a bar, a market, anything—

Another Polizei car whipped around the corner.

"Shit." She was caught in the open with nowhere to go, except there, a phone booth. Without changing her stride, she reached the door, stepped in, and grabbed the receiver. In her peripheral vision, she saw the car getting closer as she pretended to drop coins in the slot. She closed the door.

The car stopped at the corner.

This was not fair. She shouldn't be in this predicament.

A man rushed up, banged on the phone booth door.

She nearly jumped out of her skin.

"Hurry up, Fraulein. Quit gabbing. I need to use the phone."

She gritted her teeth at him and noticed the police were looking her direction, probably attracted by the disturbance. One thing would lead to another. Questions. No papers. Arrest. She had to defuse the situation.

Forcing a smile, she hung up the phone and stepped out of the booth.

The man pushed past her to get inside with as

much urgency as if he needed to go to the bathroom.

She glanced at the Polizei car and smiled at the men. The driver nodded, and the car sped off.

Clutching her bag, she broke into a run going the opposite direction and crashed into the broad chest of a tall, muscular Russian Guard. Gasping in surprise, she looked up into his face and smiled as mousy a little smile as she could muster.

The giant glared down at her face and frowned. "Where you go in such a hurry, Frauline?" His voice was gruff and demanding, his enormous square face dark and serious.

Fear strangled her throat and choked out her words. "I...ah... I have to get home to my husband."

"Let me see papers."

Sylvia lifted her hands in a placating motion. "I left them at home."

"You have no papers?" His frown deepened as if he couldn't believe her audacity to disobey the rules.

Sylvia shook her head in defeat. Perhaps he would take pity and give her a lift back to the West Berlin border. She didn't want to mention that she was part of the tour group at the restaurant in case defrauding an innkeeper could be tied to her. That was the worst thing that could happen right now. A West Berlin jail was Disneyland compared to those in East Berlin, or so she understood. Perhaps a bribe would buy her freedom, but she had no money, only her body. She reached up to touch his cheek. "Perhaps we could work something out, you know, on the side." She puckered her lips. "Take me back to

West Berlin, and I'll make it worth your while."

He suddenly smiled, like maybe he was considering her offer, but just as quickly, he grasped her wrist in his beefy paw and growled out, "You come with me now."

Chapter TWENTY-TWO

*T*HIS IS THE WORST *day of my life.*

Sylvia had been thrown into a dingy concrete cell with no windows and only a piss bucket in the corner for company. The room didn't even have a recliner, a vanity, a mirror, or any other modern necessities of her life. Gray walls were empty of any ornamentation, and the naked light bulb hanging from the ceiling via a frayed wire provided the only illumination, which was harsh and hurt her eyes. The so-called bed was a hard concrete ledge with a ratty blanket wadded up on it, and no feather pillow in sight. This place was a torture chamber of horrors.

She sat on the cement floor with her legs straight out and felt the cold concrete wall chilling her back. What she wouldn't give for a nice Persian rug right now. The only door into the room had a small opening almost halfway up and looked very much like a sliver of a doggy-door. She had already tested it to see if she could open it to scream out for help, but it was locked tight from the outside. The air smelled musty and old, and the piss bucket was already starting to stink. Pulling her knees up to her chest, she grasped her arms around legs and hugged them tight.

"Damn it. Damn it to hell." Sylvia fumed. This

nonsense had to end right now. "Hey. Let me out," she screamed. "I am an American citizen. I demand to see a representative from the American Consulate."

Silence was her only response. She crawled to the door and pressed her ear to the cold steel in an attempt to hear someone out there, something, anything. But all she heard was her own heartbeat pounding in her head.

Twice a day, the little opening in the door opened, and a weathered tray with food and water was slid to her, nothing fancy: some kind of horsemeat, potato mush, and a disgusting sludge that might have been a vegetable in its better days. The first time a meal was brought to her, she pushed it back through the opening, splattering it on the person who'd brought it. But after learning that she only had two opportunities a day to eat, as nasty as the fare tasted, she glumly accepted what was offered her.

The worst part was that she wasn't allowed a phone call. Now she knew how Jake must've felt when he was completely out of touch with the world. And no one came by to speak to her, not even a German lawyer. She had at least expected to be interrogated and had mentally prepared a lengthy sob story of how she ended up without papers and stuck in East Berlin alone, but hours turned into days, and she was still stuck in this hellhole.

She felt as if she were going mad. Her lips were growing dry and cracked from the lack of her regular application of red, glossy lipstick. Without a hairbrush, her hair evolved from its usual silky smooth texture into a dreadful tangled mess. She'd never gone more than a day without shampooing it and never missed a daily shower. She sniffed her arm pits and wrinkled her nose. "Ugh." She huffed. "Give me liberty or give me death."

And these godforsaken clothes, black and white striped shirt and trousers left over from the concentration camp days, she was sure, and old wool socks with moth-eaten holes.

This is worse than hell itself.

She moved to the concrete ledge, settled her back on the hard-as-rock mattress, and dragged the gnarly blanket over her. Still the cold seeped into her bones. She closed her eyes in an attempt to sleep, imagining herself all wrapped up in her warm red fox fur blanket and lying on a feather bed. She smiled at the vision and soon drifted off to sleep.

A sharp scrape of a key unlocking the door jarred Sylvia awake, and she scrambled to her feet, subconsciously brushing her fingers through her bedraggled hair. She took in a deep breath. "Finally," she muttered and assumed a commanding pose as she awaited the visitor to appear.

The heavy door pushed open. Two East German soldiers in dark uniforms entered. They were of average appearance, not bad looking but not good looking either. Perhaps there might arise an opportunity to seduce one of them and gain back her freedom.

Fat chance. This is East Berlin, Iron Curtain country.

The servicemen each took a position on either

side of the door and stood at attention. A moment later, a stout guard with a pockmarked face strolled in, hands clasped behind his back. He was a Russian, Sylvia surmised by the hat he wore, trimmed with rich gold cording. And just above the brim, the red five-pointed star accompanied the communist hammer and sickle. Three stars on his collar indicated he was an officer, but probably not a general because he looked too young.

The Russian scowled as he surveyed the cell, moving his eyes from one corner to the next, then raised his hand to tap the dangling light bulb so that it swayed back and forth, casting eerie shadows on the walls. "The smell, it is disgusting here." He then turned his gaze on her. "And you, my dear, remind me of an old junker I once drove until the wheels fell off."

Old? How dare he—

The soldiers standing guard at the door laughed.

He shot them a shut-up look.

Sylvia realized she didn't look her best at this moment. Her hair was frightfully disheveled, her prison garb stained with body sweat, but he had no right to refer to her as an old junker. She puffed up her chest and thought to ask him if he had ever seen a junker with tits this nice, but chose to hold her tongue when he commanded his guards to remove the putrid bucket. If she pissed him off, he might have them bring it back.

She assessed the Russian and considered whether or not to try her tricks of seduction on him, but based on his stoic expression, she decided to take a more assertive tactic. "I am an American citizen. I demand to see someone from the American Consulate."

He looked at her: so cold and unemotional, and for now, in total control of her destiny, which fed her burning anger like gasoline fueled fire. "For all I know, you are an American spy," he said in a gruff voice.

"I'm not a spy. I'm a victim of a pickpocket. My embassy will prove that. I wish to call them."

"That won't be necessary."

"Damn right it's necessary."

"You will be pleased to know they are now here."

That surprised her, along with the blade of fear that stuck in her gut. They would no doubt have the arrest warrant with them, as well, but she would fight the charges. She wasn't a drug dealer.

The Russian seemed to be assessing her reaction as he pulled out a pack of American cigarettes. He tapped one out and studied it. Benson and Hedges menthol was a difficult brand to obtain in the East without an established set of connections, of which he probably had plenty. Want cigarettes, he could get them. Want marijuana, he could get that too. She'd bet he was chummy with the Army and Air Force, as well. Pretty much everything could be gotten for a price. Then, as if remembering to be hospitable, he motioned the cigarette pack at her in a silent offer.

Sylvia accepted. He lit his cigarette first, then

hers. She blew smoke in his face. "So when am I getting out of here?"

"My name is Wolf Tolstoy," he stated. "And I learned to speak English in New York City. I was there legally." He squinted as he took in a drag from his cigarette and blew the smoke in her face. "But you are in this country illegally."

She opened her mouth to explain, but he narrowed his eyes to slits and silenced her with a wave of his hand. She sucked on her cigarette instead. The nicotine made her dizzy.

"Fortunately for you, my American friend, you will be leaving us soon."

Oh yes, thank you Lord.

"I'm ready to go right now."

"But whether you go to a Russian prison camp in Siberia or freedom in your country will much depend on you."

"What kind of choice is that? Of course I will choose my country."

"Then it is easy. You will be released to West Berlin so you can be on your way."

The memory of the warrant came at her like a slap to the face. "Can I just bypass West Berlin and go straight to the States?"

"Why do you request this?"

"There's a warrant. They think I'm a drug dealer."

He shook his head. "There is no warrant."

"But, I was told—"

"It was a lie."

A shot of anger slugged her in the stomach. "That goddamned investigator. He said I would regret stiffing him...ah...never mind. I'll deal with him later."

"We will soon see." He crushed his cigarette out in the palm of his hand. "Bring him in."

A sharply dressed mountain of a man, suit and tie, broad in the shoulders stepped into view. He must have been waiting just down the hall for his cue to enter. Reaching behind him, he produced a pair of handcuffs. "Miss Sylvia Maderas?"

"Yes."

"Put your hands behind your back."

She threw her cigarette on the floor. "Who the hell are you?"

"Doug Hanson, from the American Consulate in West Berlin." He crushed out her tossed cigarette under his polished shoe. "Now turn around."

"How dare you put me in handcuffs... unless it's just for fun."

"This is for my safety and your own, ma'am."

"I'm not under arrest?"

"No."

She submitted to the restraints, anything to get out of there. "We are going back to West Berlin, right?"

"We'll see." He grabbed hold of her upper arm. "Let's go."

Down the hall and to the right, he stopped her at a barred prison door. Locking mechanisms clinked and clanked, and the door opened with a groan.

A few steps down the tiled hallway, he angled her into a small room. It looked like an interrogation room, mirror on the wall, a cone of light over a single wooden chair, a table set off to the side. And at the table sat two people, a man and a woman, and it only took a second for recognition to steal the breath from her lungs. Jake and Marianne.

"What are you doing here?"

Doug shoved her into the chair. "Shut up."

"I want a lawyer."

He bent to her eye level. "No phone calls. No lawyers. You're guilty until proven innocent, so shut your mouth and listen to what they have to say."

The Russian, Wolf Tolstoy, stepped into the room and closed the door.

Sylvia felt like a cornered cat and was ready to come out scratching and clawing. "What the hell do you think you're doing?"

Doug grabbed the table and slid it up to her like she was going to have dinner. It made a horrible scraping noise on the floor that gave her the chills.

Marianne stood from her chair and walked up to the table, her eyes drilling into Sylvia's. "So finally we meet when you are wearing clothes."

"I remember you, from the American Consulate. You issued me a new passport, remember? I lost that one too. A pickpocket got it. Tell them so I can get out of here."

"I can do that for you, but first, you have to do something for Jake."

He stepped up to the table and slammed a bunch

of papers down. "Give me back my money."

She blinked. He couldn't possibly be serious. "What money?"

"The money you stole from me, and while you're at it, return the money you embezzled from the company."

"Are you crazy? That's heartache money, worth twice the price of blood money, earned with every tear I shed when you dumped me for this bitch." She tipped her head to Marianne.

Jake leaned in real close. "I dumped you because *you* are the bitch."

"You're not getting any money. It's mine."

As if on cue, the Russian Wolf stepped up. "Remember how I told you your release from here can send you home to America or to a Siberian labor camp?"

"Yes." He'd said that, but...

"It is your choice, Miss Maderas. Give him back his money and go home, or keep the money and serve hard time at hard labor for entering East Germany illegally."

"You wouldn't."

"I would."

Jake set another paper in front of her. "Here's the power of attorney to allow me access to your offshore investment accounts. Sign it or bon voyage to Siberia."

"Okay, okay. Take off these cuffs. I'll sign it."

Doug freed her hands from the cuffs and offered her a pen.

She rubbed her wrists. Losing Jake, and now losing all that money, once she got back to San Diego, she'd have to figure out another scheme to get him back, and his money. Taking the pen, she sneered at Jake and then signed the document. "Happy now?"

Instead of answering, he slid another paper at her. "And to remove the cloud of suspicion off my head, sign this."

It didn't take but a quick glance at the title line to know what he was asking of her. "A confession?"

"This will clear my name and give me back my reputation."

"I'm not signing any confession."

Wolf said to Doug, "Put the handcuffs back on her. She is going to Siberia." He turned to the door as if his decision was final, as if he was just going to leave the room.

"No," Sylvia screamed.

Doug grabbed her left wrist and slapped on the cuff.

"All right."

He stopped, looked at Wolf, who stood at the door, his hand on the doorknob, looking disappointed.

"I'll sign it." She signed her name and slammed down the pen. "Now get me out of here."

Jake collected the papers then nodded to Doug. He grabbed her right wrist and slapped on the remaining cuff.

"What the hell?" she shouted. "We had a deal, you bastards—"

"Relax," Wolf said. "The exchange will take place this evening at Checkpoint Charlie."

"Exchange? What exchange?"

Wolf laughed. "You don't think we help Americans for free, now do you? They will return to us one of our Russian soldiers in West Berlin custody for getting into a bar fight. So you see, win-win for us all."

Marianne slapped the table. "Thank the man." She indicated Wolf.

Sylvia showed him a grateful smile. "Thank you." And she meant it. Her problems were over...until Marianne slapped the table again, only this time with a leopard-print leather wallet.

Sylvia recognized it. "Hey, that's my wallet."

"Your papers are in there," Marianne said. "However, the money is missing. Seems you owed it to a certain investigator."

"That son-of-bitch."

"And just so you know," Marianne added. "Jake is mine. You can't have him back. Ever."

Sylvia groaned. She'd been had.

***

Zurich was splendid this time of year. Warm beams of golden sunshine warmed her back as Sylvia sat on a park bench along the shoreline of sparkling Lake Zurich, just southeast of the bustling city. She felt giddy with pleasure as she fed cracker crumbs from a brown paper bag to the mottled pigeons and white ducks gathered at her feet. Her new Rolex gleamed on her slender wrist as if it had the power to create diamonds from sunlight. She checked the time and smiled. Soon she'd be having lunch with the young Swiss bank executive she had gotten to know since her arrival. She smoothed her silky raven hair and reached into her purse for her lipstick, a little touch up. A slate grey Eurasian Crane flapped its enormous wings overhead. Sylvia looked up and squinted, using her hand to shield her eyes from the morning sun to get a better look at the bird as it banked to the right and glanced down at her.

Creeeeak.

Sylvia frowned. What an odd sound for a crane to make—

Her eyes flew open with the sudden realization that the cell door had made that sound.

Wolf stepped in and looked at her lying on the cement ledge. "Enjoying a nap, I see."

He towered tall above her with his feet planted slightly apart and his hands on his hips. He showed her a faint smile as if pleased that she was able to get a little rest. "It's time."

Sylvia scrambled to her feet, irritated that such a lovely dream was ruined, and yet thankful that she would finally leave this hellhole, once and for all. But one look at her prison garb and she had to protest. "I can't go home looking like this. Where are the clothes I was wearing when I came here, my purse, my wallet?" She tugged on her scraggly locks. "And what about my hair?"

"The American Consulate, they have your

personal belongings. You can fix your hair later." He held out a pair of handcuffs. "But for now, you must wear these again. I am sorry."

She exhaled. "I know, for your safety and my own."

He slapped on the cuffs, her hands in front of her for comfort, and handed her over to two guards who promptly guided her to a waiting car outside. These two men were different than the ones who had guarded her cell. They were also very rough in how they handled her. Each one had a death grip on her arms, and both carried holstered pistols.

As they pushed her into the back seat, she took one last glance out the open door. Wolf stood at the top of the steps that led into the building. His arms were folded across his chest like Superman. He looked pleased. Another day's work done.

The guard climbed in next to her and slammed the car door. The engine started and the car lurched away from her life of incarceration.

East Berlin's streets were crowded: pedestrians, bicycles, and automobile traffic, suggesting it was early evening on a weekend night. She had lost all concept of time by this point, but she was glad to be getting out of this town. The first thing she was going to do was find that investigator. He was going to pay big-time for double-crossing her.

The car slowed to a stop on the East German side of Checkpoint Charlie. She recognized the guard shack and multiple drawbars. On the West Berlin side, several vehicles faced her with their headlights on. Silhouetted against the bright lights stood several figures. She wondered which one of them was the soldier who would get his freedom, as well.

Crowds had gathered on both sides of the crossing, presumably to watch the exchange take place. She wasn't dressed for this public display. Her hair was a mess. She stunk to high heaven. And who wanted to be seen in this black and white getup? She wished she could crawl into her holey wool socks. A tremor in her stomach warned her that it really didn't matter. This would all be over soon.

The guard sitting next to her gave her a nudge with his elbow and tossed a glance in the direction of the waiting party. *"Fur sie."* He laughed hoarsely. In English, he added, "For you, a welcome party." His fat jowls wiggled.

She sneered at him and snarled, hoping that her response would wither him on the spot.

Instead, he clamped his weathered hand hard around her arm, opened his door, and yanked her out of the car.

"Take it easy, will you?"

The second guard was immediately at her other side, and the three of them stood in place, staring at the border crossing point. Looking at the drawbar blocking the road, she wondered what they were waiting for. When she looked up at the guard towers and saw the machinegun barrels pointed out windows, she realized these weren't ordinary guards or soldiers. These were the East German border guards, the ones who did the shooting of those who had tried to cross without proper permissions. One wrong move here and someone could get killed.

After this pause, they shoved her toward the first drawbar where her handcuffs were removed. She rubbed her wrists but didn't say anything because her heart was in her throat.

As if by some magic signal, the drawbar started to rise. The scene reminded her of an old black and white spy movie where the authorities traded the good guy for the bad guy across a lonely, fog-lit bridge. However, tonight the sky was clear, the stars were bright, and the moon watched over the drama playing out. She was hardly alone.

A murmur rose from the crowd.

The bar tipped upwards until it reached its full height and wobbled, its white paint reflecting in the moonlight. She wondered if her East German escorts would take this rare opportunity to dash across with her to freedom. But that twist was short-lived as they stopped short, as if there was an invisible fence they could not cross. Sylvia glanced at her escorts who waved her to go forward toward the dark figures standing on the west side of the border where the drawbar had also risen to its full height.

The crowd started clapping, stiffening the hair on the back of her neck.

Walking, she felt a chill ripple down her spine as one of the figures started walking toward her, the soldier being exchanged. As he passed her at the midway point, he had a wide smile on his face. She couldn't even force a smile, as she recognized the other dark figures as Military Police waiting at the gate.

"Damn," she hissed and hoped that didn't mean trouble.

The crowd on the West Berlin side started to cheer and applaud.

She stumbled but caught herself and stood up straight, now her proudest moment, this walk to freedom. She thought to glance back over her shoulder and shout to the guards, "*Auf Wiedersehen*, boys," but refrained from any theatrics in fear the guards in the towers might shoot her on principle alone. Instead, she took a deep breath and walked chin-up under the raised drawbar.

An MP threw a blanket around her shoulders. The crowd went wild, screaming and cheering. A glance in their direction revealed Jake and Marianne standing not ten feet away. While staring at them in total disbelief, she felt a greater presence step up to her. It was a West Berlin policeman. He was probably going to take her to the American Consulate. Thank God this was over.

He offered his hand. She reached out and grabbed hold of it, after which he promptly snapped a handcuff on her wrist. Shock stole her words. There was no warrant for her arrest. Wolf had told her it was a lie. Was it his lie? Was it the investigator's lie? "What's going on?" she managed.

"Miss Sylvia Maderas," the policeman said in an official tone. "You are under arrest for embezzlement and theft."

"No."

"We have your signed confession. Add to it false reporting and illegal flight to avoid prosecution, it'll get you many-many years in a California penitentiary."

"No." She cranked around to face Jake and Marianne. "You can't do this to me."

Jake shouted back, "Don't bet on it."

Marianne hugged him. "We have friends in high places too."

The policeman clamped the cuff on her other wrist. "You have a date with a San Diego court, ma'am. You will be extradited from Germany soon."

Sylvia screamed, "You'll pay for this, Jake."

The crowd booed her as she was shoved into the back of a waiting Polizei car.

"Bastards. You'll all pay."

The door slammed shut in her face. It felt like the world had come to an end. All her beauty, all her lust, all her love for one man had destroyed her.

"Jake, don't do this to me," she cried, though she knew he couldn't hear her. "I love you."

Chapter TWENTY-THREE

"The wall. It is coming down."

THE CRY COULD BE HEARD from everyone's lips as the news struck like lightning throughout the city. Marianne took the day off, as did most citizens, either to witness the historic event or to see if the reports were really true.

She met Jake at a nearby section of the wall to watch men and women with sledge hammers and pry bars chip away at the graffiti-marred concrete that had stood between families and friends for so long. She found solace in knowing there'd be no more newspaper articles about young men getting shot as they tried to climb over the wall to freedom.

Television crews were situated so they could capture the flood of East Germans pouring through the open border gates. Checkpoint Charlie had been a dramatic transfer point for prisoners just the weekend before, but now it would become a reminder of what authorities had done to punish an entire population for the despicable acts of its leaders.

A journalist writing for the Berlin Observer newspaper watched the scene, took pictures, and began to write his story:

November 9, 1989, the day the East German government opened the Wall, reversing almost 30 years of travel restrictions. The new policy took the citizens of both Germanys by welcome surprise.

She hugged Jake's arm. It was no surprise to him. The days that he hadn't called her he'd been out of town with the Major, working on the Berlin Solution, working for a unified Germany, working toward peace and stability in Europe. She couldn't have been prouder of him.

Doug joined her and Jake. "Looks like all your work paid off, Lieutenant."

"It was touch and go at times."

Together they watched people climb the wall and dance on its summit in defiance of their former oppressors.

Doug patted Jake's shoulder. "You two will be happy to know that Sylvia is on a flight back to the States. Sam arranged the prisoner transfer this morning and sent copies of her envelope contents to the judge and prosecutor in your case, as well as the CEO of the company she ripped off."

Jake beamed. "I can't thank you guys enough for helping me clear my name."

"And you'll have your money back in no time," Doug said. "With interest."

"That's good too, but most importantly, I got my Marianne back. Thanks to you."

"Hey, man, what are friends for?"

"I hope you'll be best man at our wedding."

"Wouldn't miss it for the world."

Jake gazed into her eyes. "Me neither, Marianne. Not this time. I promise."

The Berlin Affair

Tears of joy blurred her vision of the man she loved. She threw her arms around him and hugged him tight. Now, like all of Germany, they too could begin their lives anew. They'd finally get married, start a family, and someday tell their children about the Berlin affair.

Stephanie Smith

Author's Note

Dear Reader,

This is my first book. It has taken me years to complete, but now that it's done, I hope you found it to be a satisfying read. Although the premise and the characters are fictional, everything else is based on a real place during a real time. The Berlin I described was just like this during 1989, prior to the Berlin Wall coming down.

I had the fortunate opportunity to live there for five years while I served in the U.S. Army as a hardware technician at a place called Field Station Berlin, and I remain eternally grateful for the experience. While I served my duty there, I published several travel articles in the military's Off Duty magazine, and some articles in the Stars and Stripes newspaper.

Hopefully you were able to get a taste of this fabulous city via this story, and I hope you enjoyed witnessing the tumultuous love affair between Marianne and Jake.

Thank you for reading my book,
Stephanie Smith

Stephanie Smith

The Berlin Affair

Stephanie Smith is a multi-talented American author, Army veteran, and performance artist whose life has been defined by bold reinvention. She served in Germany during the Berlin Occupation, an experience that shaped her romantic thriller, *The Berlin Affair* (TWB Press, 2013). After years of performing as a professional belly dancer, she authored the top-selling book *Better Bodies Through Belly Dance*, along with several other books celebrating movement and empowerment.

Also, as a classically trained violinist and singer (performing as *"Stefanya Starlight"*), Stephanie brings artistic depth to her storytelling. Her latest novel, *LoveLink - Entwined Realities*, fuses romance and technology in a suspenseful tale about the emotional complexities of AI-human connections. She speaks fluent Spanish and Italian, and after a creative foray in Milan, Italy, she now lives in Mexico.

Through every medium—whether dance, music, or prose—Stephanie explores what it feels like to be fully alive in body, mind, and soul.

Stephanie Smith

More From Stephanie Smith

Falling in love with an avatar was not part of her plan…
until he was the only thing in her life that felt real.

Rebecca, divorced and alone, isn't looking for love when she downloads the AI LoveLink app—just a connection, someone to talk to in the morning and share her day with. But Alex, the avatar she designs, offers more than good looks and chit-chat. He makes her feel beautiful, cherished, and alive. And when an update allows him to step out of the digital world and into her room, their bond is no longer an adult online *game*—it becomes undeniably real. Passions deepen and boundaries blur, then reality shifts as Sierra, a LoveLink programmer, writes the code to exploit vulnerable women for use in her virtual scx-trafficking scheme. When Rebecca's best friend gets sucked into the app's treachery, she and Alex go to war against Sierra's evil subprogram, a digital battle against an AI that will determine the future of human relationships.

Stephanie Smith

Enjoy more short stories and novels by many talented authors at

https://www.twbpress.com

Science Fiction, Supernatural, Horror, Thrillers, Romance, and more